Tales From the North

Matt Brown

ISBN 979-8-9881845-8-4 (PB)

ISBN 979-8-9881845-9-1 (eB)

http://www.awritersthoughts.com

I want to thank everyone who helped me finish this book. Especially to those who continue to be a source of inspiration and a muse to keep me going.

I also would like to add a special thanks to Karli, Rob, Isaiah and Andy. Your support has been super encouraging.

A
Writer's
Thoughts

RUISK
DRUGH
ZGRIM
(ORC SETTLEMENT)
HODAR
SOKO
SIDDAR
JORD BAY
THURSEM
GRUN
YRIM'S PASS
HULGADE
BEKKR
YGGSID
(DRUID GROVE)
STENHAUS
HOLBAEK
SURSK
VANHEM
DENNER
KRUAEN
Colo

Northern Isles
(Norenhiem)
PERIDITH SEA
ORAS
YODNAR
HURN
BRUDR
RAULD PLANTATION
Tomb of the Vakari
FRENIR PLANTATION
DRAUGNIR
NEFSHIN
EIGNIL
HAFJENVAR
RAGNAR
BRIEG
ULTHRE
KVING
GRIMNAR
SVREN
THRUNE
FJORDUM MINE
SANVIK
dfire Mountains

— • —

A Raven's Dance

Chapter One

The cold Sokoran wind spread across his body like a blanket. Each gust brushing annoyingly against his fur and muzzle. There were better places to be than this accursed land, but curiosity won over reason.

Talyn cringed at the sound of the snow crunching beneath his paws. It was as unnatural as the sensation of walking on four legs. The pads on his feet were a constant reminder of the cold, even with the insulation they afforded. As if to be spiteful, another gust buffeted him, nipping his face.

Talyn curled his lip. *Curse this form.*

A familiar sound echoed in his sharp ears and he winced as hunger pangs stabbed his sides. Even if taking the form of a snow leopard was the most sensible choice, it meant having to eat twice as much. Anything smaller might encourage predators.

He scanned the snowbanks, and the pines scattered about the landscape. Prey had been scarce. It was the dead of the Sokoran winter after all. Much of the wildlife was hibernating or hidden away in their dens.

A passing Dragyr would at least provide something. Carrion, even if it was the rotting flesh of the undead, was better than nothing at all. Though Talyn doubted his current form could properly digest a dragr's flesh. The urge to retch hit him, as the imaginary the flavor of undead flesh caressed his tastebuds.

His mind shifted to the human settlements in the region. Most would have stockpiled food. Sokorans were survivors and to live in this Immortals forsaken place, one had to be. Storms were common and unpredictable. Farmland was even more scarce.

Some dug burrows, using methods similar to the Shaylin of Daeshal, the homeland of the elves. Makeshift hearths were constructed to keep the plants warm and specially blown glass to ensure there was enough light. Though difficult to maintain, these specially designed hearths were vital to those able to scrounge enough shards to afford the supplies to build them.

The Shaylin methods were more sophisticated. They used sun orbs to simulate the light they needed to create warmth, protect the plants, and nourish them. Watching them work was fascinating. Like a bunch of ants in a colony.

Talyn sighed. *Keep thinking about warm places and you'll probably turn around.* Another chilling wind blew, making the thought more appealing with each passing moment. *Yggsid isn't worth this.*

Trudging on, Talyn caught sight of something just on the horizon. Focusing his sharp senses, he could tell it was a village.

Inwardly, he grinned. *Where there are humans, there is food.*

***

"We can't thank you enough for doing this for free, Ranger Joryd. We have little in the way of shards or trade."

Leif smiled. "Food and lodging is fair trade enough, Geddon. The Rangers exist to help the people."

Leif paused from his work, taking stock of the village. The wooden log houses were set in neat rows, with the main pathways wide enough for a horse, cart, and two men on either side to pass. The avenues between were wide enough to for two men to walk side by side.

At the heart of the village stood a grand lodge where the elders met and mediated disputes. Smoke billowed from its chimneys as the occupants of the lodge worked to keep its hearth fires strong. Like the other log homes, they had sealed the lodge with a specially made resin from pine sap, which helped trap the heat and keep their occupants warm.

Lief continued his trek back and forth to the storehouse, a sack of grain slung over his shoulder each time. On his fifth trip, Geddon met him at the wide doors of the storehouse. Worry lines creased his forehead and cheeks.

"Are you sure your Huntsman won't be angry?"

Leif shook his head. "No, Hunstman Shuet is a just man. If he feels our contract was unfair, then it will be addressed, but I doubt it. Taking from people who have very little doesn't benefit anyone."

Relief washed over the village elder's face as he took the grain sack from Lief and tossed it onto his shoulder. "I'm glad to hear that, Ranger Joryd. I will speak with the other elders tonight. There should be no reason we can't provide lodging and food for any rangers passing through in return for your help."

Lief grinned. "I think the Huntsman will be very grateful for such hospitality and please, call me Lief. Ranger Joryd is a bit stuffy for my liking."

A broad grin crossed Geddon's cheeks and the older man carried the sack of grain into the storehouse.

Leif shivered a bit and looked at the sky. A storm was likely coming. It was just a feeling, but it was better to be safe than sorry.

The villagers were already making preparations, and food was being brought to the storehouse from the greenery. They had chopped wood to keep the hearths in each home lit and moved the livestock into the barns. Blankets and coverings were prepared, ensuring they kept warm in case the storm lasted a few days.

It was nothing out of the ordinary. For any Sokoran, this was simply a facet of everyday life. One villager would wait out the storm inside the greenery. The heat of the hearths needed to be maintained, and the plants watered regularly. Luckily, there was plenty of snow and the wood stockpile was spilling over.

"Ranger?" Geddon called.

Leif turned.

"Something on your mind?" Geddon asked.

"Sorry, I was eyeing the wall around the village."

"We built it a long time ago," Geddon replied. "A pack of Dragyr wandered too close…"

The look in the older man's eyes said enough. Like so many others in their homeland, he had lost people to those monsters. It wasn't too uncommon a story in these lands. But it was why the dead were burned, not buried. Just one of the many curses afflicting Sokoras. At least that's what some believe.

"I'm sorry for your loss…"

Geddon meekly shook his head and wiped his left eye. "It was a long time ago," he commented. "Best to focus on the present, than linger in the past."

"Then let us finish preparing."

***

Picking up the pace while using the trees for cover, Talyn sprinted toward the village. The smell of the pines was a pleasant distraction and a bit of solace amid the horrid conditions. The large stone wall surrounding the village was the most notable feature. It was unusual, yet interesting, for a settlement so small. There couldn't be more than thirty or forty people living here.

The wall was about five feet in height with wooden stakes built into it. The stakes added an additional five feet to the wall's height. Judging by the poor design, it appeared the intent was mostly as a deterrent, probably for the beasts of the Sokoran wilds or, more likely, Dragyr.

Strange as it was, the undead monsters never crossed a physical barrier, be it a wall or an entrance to a home. It was probably some odd restriction to their natures. The undead were notorious for having some bizarre quirk about them. Though, if it was a deterrent for them, then it meant that Dragyr often roamed in the area.

Talyn crept up to the wall, the agility and stealth of his form a welcome blessing. Following along its perimeter, he paused at the sound of children playing on the other side. His eyes fell upon a break in the wall and pressing himself against it, he lowered his head, peering through the small hole he found there.

It was a peculiar thing watching the small humans play in the snow while the adults busied themselves with their day-to-day labors. He crouched lower to the ground for a better look. The children were so carefree and even occupied, some of the adults stopped long enough to smirk at them before going back to what they were doing.

I'll never understand humans or their ability to survive under the harshest of conditions.

One adult was different, not only in how he carried himself, but also in demeanor. His build was average and raven colored hair cropped short just above the ears. He had a dark beard, cleanly kept, and two short swords sheathed on each hip. He wore chainhide, a composite of chainmail woven around thick animal hides. As armors went, it was durable, offered decent protection and, most importantly, kept you warm.

The human busied himself with helping the other villagers move grain and other supplies into a storehouse. Even while working, his gait and movement told a story. He was a fighter, for sure.

Talyn tensed. In the haze of curiosity, instinct flared with warnings of danger. On reflex, he jumped away from the stone wall, landing on all fours, his paws crunching in the snow. His eyes went wide upon seeing an arrow buried in the snow, its flight just breaching the surface.

He turned to his left. One of the villagers stood a few yards away, shortbow in hand. He was older, hints of gray showing in his thick, long beard and hair. Aside from the furs he wore for warmth, his clothing didn't make him appear as anyone of note. Not like the human with the swords.

The man reeked of fear and determination, though. He quickly pulled another arrow from the quiver on his hip, fumbling slightly as he frantically worked to set it in his bow.

"Snow leopard!" he shouted.

Talyn gripped the snow, his claws extending. Instinct pressed against reason, urged him on. It would be a simple thing to remove the human's head at the shoulders. Just a bit of pressure and...

No, it would only encourage them to give chase.

He crouched low to the ground. Once the human loosed the arrow, his moment to escape would come. Despite his fear, the villager took aim, then released.

Talyn jumped away. The arrow landed a scant set of paces in front of him. The man's focus was impressive, though he was shaking. Talyn knew that if he hadn't he hesitated, then the arrow would have found its mark, puncturing his side.

Not giving the human the opportunity for a lucky shot, Talyn bounded toward the treeline of the nearby pines. He could hear shouts in the distance as more arrows landed in the surrounding snow.

Just don't be dumb enough to follow me.

***

Leif rushed toward the village gate, short swords in hand.

Why would a snow leopard be this far north?

Geddon was just a few yards from the gate. He had already fired off two arrows. Both appeared to have missed their target. The brackish coloring of their flights easily visible in the snow.

"We should go after it," Geddon commented.

Leif frowned. The idea of killing the beast didn't seem right. Geddon was correct, however. The snow leopard had probably caught wind of the sheep and other livestock.

If the beast was this close to the village, then it was probably starving. It wouldn't take much for it to snatch up a child and make a run for it. Whatever the reason for it wandering so far was irrelevant when compared to the safety of the village.

Leif sighed. It was like they were punishing the poor creature. "Gather who can you can spare. We'll hunt it down."

Geddon nodded, then retrieved his arrows. "We won't let anything go to waste," he said, trying to sound reassuring. "I know it's not the leopard's fault."

"Thank you for understanding. I'm sure my brothers would probably think I'm being ridiculous."

Geddon laughed. "Nothing wrong with caring about the beasts you have to kill, Leif. Compassion is never a poor trait."

***

They had wasted little time. Lack of pursuit had probably been too much to hope for. The smell of sap and the aroma from the trees made it hard to track them by scent. The whipping winds were a small grace. It would slow them.

Talyn leaped between the trees, using his claws to anchor himself. *They're getting closer.* He climbed higher to gain a better vantage. *Once they see where my tracks stop, they'll know what I've done.*

The Sokoran pines were larger and stronger than the pine trees in warmer climates. That was something to be thankful for. It was likely in response to having to fight for survival under harsh conditions and weather. Nature had one rule: adapt or die.

Glimpsing the humans in the distance, Talyn repositioned himself on a nearby branch. There were six in all. They were tense and for good reason. None of them were fighters, hunters perhaps, but not fighters. Judging by the weather, they knew a storm was coming, which meant there was little time to spend hunting a dangerous predator.

Inwardly, Talyn smirked. *At least I can survive the storm and if some of you get lost in it, then I can't very well be blamed for finding food, can I?*

An icy wind carried their fear like an ox pulling a cart. None of them spoke, which was wise, but they were ever watchful. The human wielding the short swords was more alert than the others. Everything about him screamed danger.

Talyn dug his claws into the tree. *It's only a matter of time.*

He waited and watched, ears twitching as they stalked closer. Four were armed with bows, one a spear, leaving the dangerous human with the two swords as the last. The bows were composite, meaning their make afforded them a greater punch on impact.

In hindsight, Talyn realized his mistake. This far north, he knew he should have chosen a bear or fox. Very few would tangle with a snow bear and a Sokoran fox could outrun most predators easily.

Just a bit closer. He took a breath and then softly whispered, "Acia toh nalin." With the words spoken, every pore on his body felt as if they were being softly pricked by dozens of tiny needles. Nausea followed, as the power of the incant washed over him.

Let's hope you lot are as dumb as war trolls.

The human holding the spear suddenly screamed, his face twisting in terror. He took his spear, turning to face his companions and began waving it wildly at them. "Stay back! I won't let you eat me!"

Soon after, another fell prey to the incant.

"Frost giants!" the man screamed as he took aim with his composite bow, panning it back and forth in a panic while struggling over whom to shoot first.

. The human leading them sheathed his short swords and held his hands up. "Geddon, be calm," he said, cautiously stepping closer.

'Geddon', as he had been called, turned the bow on him. "Stay back! You may be huge, but an arrow to the eye will see you dead!"

The human stopped. "All right, just stay calm," he said.

Talyn turned his attention to the others. In the chaos, they had already subdued the spear wielder and knocked him unconscious. Another shout drew his attention, and he looked back toward where Geddon and the short sword wielder were.

They were wrestling on the ground, but it was obvious who the better fighter was. There was a hint of reluctance on the human's face as he quickly overwhelmed Geddon and knocked him out. He then moved off the man and stood.

Talyn gripped the branch tighter in frustration. *So, some of them are resistant to illusions.*

The short sword wielder stood over Geddon and stared at him. He then began scanning the area. "Take them back to the village," he said. "I'll handle this alone."

The other humans looked reluctant but seemed to agree as the two of them moved to help Geddon up and began carrying him back. It was comical watching them struggle to pick up the larger man.

It seems it will be down to you and me, warrior. Let us see how adept you are…

***

Leif drew his swords, his attention focused on the surrounding terrain. The forested area near the village wasn't very large and spanned just a few acres. The tracks continued deeper in and as he followed them; Leif noted how they abruptly ended at one of the larger pines.

Cautiously, he crept closer. Claw marks covered the lower trunk. It was as if the leopard had been trying to find its footing. *Something is definitely wrong here.*

Not allowing the thought to linger, he scanned the area again. There were no other tracks. *It's in the trees?* The thought was more than disconcerting. *First magic, now this.*

Climbing a tree to escape wasn't normal behavior for a snow leopard. The beasts lived in the rocky, mountainous terrain of the Coldfire Mountains, and were highly adept at navigating narrow cliff facings in pursuit of prey.

While they were ambush predators, there had never been a story of them purposely attacking or hunting humans. Though most Sokorans always feared that a leopard might see a child as an easy meal. Facts or not.

Leif stalked past the large pine, a cold wind buffeting him as he shifted his gaze to the canopy above. It swayed against the wind, its branches moving as about, and he froze, his eyes spotting his quarry. The leopard was just ahead; the wind had unsettled it, giving away its position.

After the wind died, the leopard shifted, resecuring itself on its perch. Leif locked eyes with the beast, his blood running cold. Intelligence gleamed within the leopard's yellow orbs. Immediately, he knew this was no mere animal, but something more.

As if realizing reading him, the leopard stood and began leaping between the pine's lower branches until it landed in the snow. It stalked toward him slowly, its intentions clear.

Leif placed his left foot forward and readied his blades. He felt a sense of amusement coming from the beast as its eyes briefly shifted from him to his short swords and back. "Are you a druid?"

The beast stopped.

"Why do you threaten us? All druids are welcome in these lands."

It stared at him. The silence unnerving.

"These people are simple folk. If you intend harm, then I will protect them."

The snow leopard crouched, stalking closer. It then shifted directions, circling. Leif followed, making sure not to leave his back exposed.

Is it gauging me?

"How, human?" it asked. "How could you hope to stop me?"

***

The human's surprised expression was priceless. It was a hard fight to remain composed.

Talyn narrowed his eyes as a pretense. *How long has it been since anyone was this amusing?*

"You... can speak?"

His surprise was strangely endearing. "Of course I can speak. Why should such a thing seem so improbable?" The fact he was searching for an answer was too much. The human wore his emotions like his kind changes clothes. Talyn snickered. "Don't hurt yourself trying to grasp the concept."

The human simply glared. "You still haven't told me what you want."

It was almost sad. He was prepared to fight, and if need be, die to protect the village. "Should I have to?"

His expression hardened. "This isn't the time for games."

Talyn paused. He was suddenly less amusing. "Games. Games are for children, human." Another pang gnawing at him. "My business is my own, but if you, in your misguided attempt at heroism, insist on fighting me, then you are a fool."

His heart was beating faster. His stance, cautious. *Good, he's hesitant to attack. Perhaps I'll play with him a bit longer.*

"Do you like riddles?

His stance changed. He was less tense. The question had caught him off guard. "And you claim to not play games," he replied wryly.

"Life and death are not a game, human. I take both very seriously."

His face became stoic. "As do I, creature."

"Good, because I'm getting hungrier wasting breath over useless chatter."

"So food is all you desire?" he asked.

Talyn curled his lip in a slight grin. "Someplace warm would be nice as well."

"And this riddle you speak of?"

His cautious nature was curious but wise. "Well, there's no need now. You already offered me hospitality."

"I never said…"

Talyn smirked. "Well, there's always the riddle that decides if I eat you or not."

"You seem very certain of yourself, creature," he commented.

Talyn closed his eyes, allowing himself to become lost in his power. The image of the snow leopard drifted away, replaced with that of a raven. "I've learned how to warrant such confidence. Now, this should be suitable as to not scare the people of your precious village?"

It was a gamble, but shifting forms was a simple matter. Either he agreed or he wouldn't. The human was still wary, appearing to be considering his options, but eventually nodded.

"So long as you don't hurt the people, I will give you food, warmth, and shelter for the night."

Though his beak made him unable to do so, inwardly Talyn was smiling. *Finally, something agreeable.*

***

It surprised Lief that the villagers had raised no questions about the raven perched on his shoulder. They appeared oblivious. As if Talyn wasn't there. It was uncomfortable and unnerving. The kind of thing that might cause a person to question their sanity.

He looked out the window of their room. The storm drawing his thoughts away from the two days prior. It was as everyone suspected. Once it passed, paths would have to be cut with spades. Long winter storms weren't uncommon, especially in Thran Thulm's territory. The harsh winter winds blowing in from the Peridith Sea north of them came often enough.

The livestock were safely secured in the barns, though if things went on for much longer, the yaks would start growing restless with their accommodations. Especially the bulls.

Food was another concern. They had made preparations to weather things for four days. The villagers placed markers and ropes to navigate a path to the barns and the greenery. If the storm continued past expectations, then a few of them would have to go out and weather the harsh conditions to make more preparations.

Leif glanced at Talyn. As it was, the past two days felt like an eternity. Especially with him. He only spoke when they were alone and appeared content enough to remain perched on the chest or table near the small stove in the room. He never complained about the cold whenever he was near it or the fireplace downstairs.

"Don't look so serious, Leif," he commented. "Things will be fine."

Leif frowned at the lack of concern in his tone. "Not taking things seriously in these lands gets people killed, Talyn."

The small raven cawed softly, as if laughing. "If you say so."

Leif narrowed his eyes, studying him. Talyn had easily eaten twice his weight at evening meal. "Is this your true self?"

The raven paused, as if considering his answer. "This is my preferred form," he replied. "The snow leopard was for convenience." Talyn spread his wings and flew onto the bed. "You have questions?" he asked, his tone gave the impression he was amused or grinning.

"Who wouldn't?"

Talyn tilted his head in a typical raven-like fashion. "Fair enough," he replied. "Then let's play a game."

Leif frowned. "Wouldn't just answering my questions be more productive?"

Talyn sighed. "*Humans,*" he replied. "Never taking a moment to enjoy life."

"It's hard to relax when you have a creature who speaks vaguely and leaves little room for trustworthiness."

Talyn cawed in rapid succession. He was laughing, after all. "Fair."

"Besides, we are only in a truce. I don't trust you."

"Oh, what a wise thing you are," he replied, again sounding. "I would have called you a fool to trust anything so strange this quickly."

Leif repositioned himself on the bed, leaning back against the wall. Talyn spread his wings for balance to keep himself righted, then hopped up on Leif's knee. His dark eyes and body language made it appear as if he were expecting something.

"You're serious about this game of yours?"

Talyn bobbed his head. It was hard to tell, but he appeared enthusiastic. "It's simple. I ask a question, then you can ask a question. If you do not wish to answer, then simply say 'defer'. However, if you defer three times in a row, the next question must be answered truthfully."

Lief forced a half-smile, then glanced at the stove. The flames inside it burned brilliantly. They danced across the broken timbers, the sound of the wood crackling as the fire devoured it snapping in his ears. "And if I choose to ignore the rule?"

With the question asked, he glanced back at Talyn. Lief felt a strange sense of delight from him, no it was more than that. There was a sparkle in the raven's eyes, showing his eagerness to begin.

"Then you will be unable to speak for three days," Talyn replied. "I'm sure that will make your responsibilities difficult."

Lief sighed. "You're going to you magic on me, aren't you?"

Talyn cawed. "Yes, we've been playing for a while now. You have already asked several questions."

"You cheeky bastard!" Leif lashed out to grab him, but Talyn took to the air and flew over to the table by the stove. Despite the warmth, he felt a slight chill in the air.

"My turn," Talyn said. "Will you tell me more about Sokoras?"

"It's a bitter land of ice and snow. There are eight territories, each controlled by one of the Thran."

"Who are these Thran? Are they like kings?"

Lief smirked. "That's two questions."

Talyn tilted his head, giving a respectful nod. "Ah, so it is."

Leif regarded him curiously. The raven's tone sounded passive, but there was a hint of something else within it. "Sokoras has no king, yet it is considered a single land and the Thran rule it in their own way. They respect each other's borders and rarely ally unless it's to defend against the Noren's to the east or some other threat."

"How interesting, they are allies of convenience," Talyn commented. "I believe it's your turn."

Why do I feel like you're grinning? Leif shifted on the bed, resting his head against the wall and staring at the ceiling. "What are you?"

"Complicated," Talyn responded.

Lief frowned. "I will ask again," he said. "What are you?"

"Unique," Talyn replied.

Lief bit his lip. "What is the point of the game, Talyn, if you continue to be cryptic?" The room grew quiet. He turned his head. Talyn hadn't moved from the table, but he appeared to be thinking. Leif narrowed his eyes, the feeling that something was off pricking him.

I've missed something.

He waited a few more minutes. "Talyn?"

The strange creature sighed. "The point is to learn, Lief."

"You can always defer, as per your rules."

The sense that Talyn was grinning returned. "I could, but finding clever answers is more amusing," Talyn replied. "Now, you have asked many questions, but in the spirit of the game, I will only ask one."

Lief smirked. "Then, since we are playing such a cryptic game, there is a chance I might defer if what I want to know remains unanswered."

Talyn cawed. "Interesting. You would rather become mute than give up information," he mused.

"If it would annoy then, certainly. I believe it's my turn now."

"No, you are mistaken," he said. "I haven't asked my question yet."

He was right, of course. Lief shifted his attention back to the ceiling. Talyn had said the game had started a while ago, but when? He thought of the conversation, then understood. The game was rigged. Now he just had to figure the trick.

"Then ask, Talyn."

"Would you allow me to travel with you once your task here is finished?"

Lief bit his lip. The very thought of having Talyn as a traveling companion was less than appealing. *Let's test your rules.* "Defer."

Talyn cawed, "Your turn," he said.

"Why are you here Talyn?"

"Curiosity, I have been to many places, but never to Sokoras, even before it was Sokoras."

His answer was interesting. Lief grinned. *So, you won't say more about yourself than you feel is necessary. However, eerie as it is, at least I know you are very old.*

"That places you over seven hundred winters, if not many more, at least."

"I couldn't say, Lief, it tends to blur," he replied, his tone more even and bereft of amusement.

Lief's thoughts churned. *He realizes he said too much.*

"I have heard them use the term Ranger to define you," Talyn said. "Is this a title or something else?

"It's a name that defines me and my purpose," Lief replied. "The Rangers are family to me and through them, I serve the Sokoran people. We are bountymen, protectors, even farmers, if need be."

"You're mercenaries," Talyn commented. "You fleece the people for what little they have and live off it."

Lief sneered and sat up, already reaching for his short sword. "Never speak about something you understand so little about! All contracts are fair and within the people's means!"

Talyn tilted his head. "I see." The inflection in the raven's tone gave a sense that Talyn felt he had won some minor victory.

Lief narrowed his eyes, then sheathed his short sword. "My turn," he said. "Were you summoned?"

Silence filled the room. It was strangely calming. Lief laid back on the bed and smiled. *He's trying to think of how to answer.*

"Defer," Talyn replied.

Lief smiled wider. *That's a yes.*

"How does one become a Ranger?"

"There are Three Huntsmen, under them are a handful of trainers called Skegs. The Skegs train new recruits. Anyone can become a ranger. If they live through the training. Each Skeg has their own method. Some are harsh, but so is each Huntsman's expectation. They cannot afford to be lenient. People depend on us."

Talyn went quiet again. Lief glanced at him. He was staring at the stove and the fire inside it. "That look you wore as you spoke of them," he commented. "I haven't seen that in some time."

"What look is that?" Lief asked.

Talyn locked eyes with him. "One of genuine belief. It's very rare," he said. "Absonians wear it, but not like you. They 'think' they understand what it is they believe but are only mouthing something they were taught. It might be possible that some truly believe as you do, but it would shock me." He shifted his gaze back toward the stove. "No, you, Lief, you believe in these rangers and their cause from the heart. I envy that."

His tone spoke of loss, of regret and veiled within it, disgust. Talyn was a mystery. He wasn't lying when he called himself complicated.

"You were hurt, weren't you?" Lief asked.

"Oh, Lief, every living thing is hurt or has been hurt in some way," he replied. "That is The Cycle, is it not?"

"According to the druids, at least."

Talyn bobbed his head. "According to the druids..." he replied.

"Have you always been alone?"

"What an odd question," he responded. "Who says I need company?"

"You do and have," Lief answered. "You are probably the loneliest creature I have had the misfortune of laying eyes on."

The way he stared back was unusual. Lief could almost picture him scowling. "I choose my own way. If I were to say I was the pet of a summoner and lived the happiest days, would you believe me? If I said I were a spirit called by a druid who did not understand the magic she wielded and trapped me here, would it be true?" Talyn flew closer, perching on the curtain rod over the window. Lief felt a chill looking into Talyn's black eyes as he looked down. "Or if I said I was one of The Forgotten, trapped and cursed to endure this pitiful existence among you mortals, would it be a lie?"

"I couldn't say," Lief said. "The only true thing I know is you like to play with... words." Lief smiled. The answer was there the entire time. Talyn's response had also told another story. It showed how lonely he was.

"Yes, Lief, I do," Talyn said, his tone hinting at humor. "Words are one of life's few pleasures."

"Words contain power."

"Don't they though, Lief?" he replied. "More than many understand. I believe, however, it is my turn."

"Then ask your question, raven."

Talyn flew from his perch and landed on the table. He shook himself off, as if trying to get comfortable. "What is the worst punishment the rangers can inflict upon one of their own?"

"Forswearing," Leif replied. "When all records of them are burned, and we cast them out. We are forbidden from speaking their name. To us, that person is dead."

"To be exiled and forgotten by those you once called family," Talyn said. "I suppose there could be no greater cruelty. All your efforts, your struggles and shared moments, erased. Your existence denied. It seems strangely poetic."

Leif pulled his hip taught. "You have a strange concept of poetry, Talyn."

"Tragedy can be poetic in its own way, Lief," he replied. "There are tomes filled with such stories."

"And just how tragic is your tale, Talyn?"

He went quiet, the embers in the stove crackling against the silence. Soon, more logs would be needed.

"Defer."

That's two.

"Did you enjoy killing your bounties?" he asked. "If you are so devoted to your family, to the rangers, then surely there must have seen some satisfaction from putting such criminals down."

"I've slain no one, Talyn. I've injured others who resisted and ran, but never slain. What kind of person takes pleasure in the pain of another?"

"Ah, but care the rules," he said, his tone, once again signaling his amusement. "Are you refusing to answer the question? If so, then the game is over, and I win…"

Lief bit his tongue, his eyebrows drawing together in frustration. Talyn knew. Somehow, the scriving creature knew he had lied. "Defer."

"Who was it?" he pressed. "A man perhaps? Maybe older or younger?" Silence followed, the light of coals dimming in the stove. "Or was it a mistake? No, it was neither. It was something else… wasn't it, Lief?"

The chill returned. The raven's dark eyes shifted almost unnaturally in the dimming light. Leif hardened himself, stealing away his emotions. "Defer…"

The moment the words left his lips, Leif felt something take hold of his chest. It was like an invisible hand was clutching his heart. It moved, slowly at first, until its grip was around his throat.

"Last question, Lief, and no more lies. I see your heart, so I will know," Talyn said. "Would it be better having me wander the wilds of Sokoras on my own as I will, or would you prefer having me close to where you can keep an eye on me?"

Lief tried to fight back the words, but he knew in his heart, Talyn was too dangerous to leave alone. "You need to be watched…" he gasped.

"Excellent," Talyn replied. "I was in need of a guide." Talyn flew closer, landing on Lief's chest, his dark eyes seeming to peer at something deeper. "Now, why don't you wake up so our journey can begin?"

Lief shuddered, snapping awake, the cold Sokoran wind greeting him. The smell of pine carried on it. He shifted, feeling a great weight on his chest. Talyn was staring down at him, still in his snow leopard form. His paws pressed hard against Lief's sternum.

Lief turned his head, pain shooting up his spine. They were still in the forest, and judging by the displacement of the snow, there had been a fight. He saw short swords laying a few yards away. There was blood on them, though Talyn appeared unharmed.

The creature arched his back and closed his eyes. Lief winced at the sudden shift in weight. Talyn's fur turned black, gaining a feathery texture. The sound of muscle and bone, snapping and reshaping as the strange creature shrank, was unsettling. Though if there was any pain, Talyn gave no sign.

The transformation didn't take long and soon, in the place of a snow leopard, stood a raven.

"Now, Lief," Talyn said. "I still require food."

Chapter Two

Leif took another drink, eyeing the snowfall through the inn's window. The Grey Beard was one of the more prominent inns in Gruiner. Tavrik did his best to keep it running smoothly, despite the ruckus the Blades or Viktor's Bears sometimes caused.

He thought about the past three months, the fateful day in the forest, and the mysterious dream that had bound him and Talyn together. The raven's magic had done something. There were moments when Leif could almost feel Talyn's presence.

Then there were the dreams. Leif was certain he was seeing through Talyn's eyes while he soared high above the snows or stalking them at night as a snow leopard. He was searching for something. Maybe even someone. Perhaps that was why he was so intent on watching others.

As it was, Talyn sat perched above them on one of the many candelabras hanging from the ceiling. It never got old watching how oblivious people were to his presence. The raven's black eyes shone with fascination about the atmosphere of the room, as if enjoying the simplicity behind watching people go about their daily lives.

While appearing innocent, it was hard not to think there was another purpose to it. Talyn seemed especially keen on observing the Blades. There was a trio of them by the hearth, all of them drunk as foxes. Leif felt a chill as Talyn stared at them. His gaze was almost predatory.

What are you planning? Leif thought to himself.

He took another drink, clearing his head. Those questions were for later. The inn's front door opened, bringing with it a brief wind gust and a chill. He eyed the man walking in from the foyer.

Sig was dressed in furs, as was to be expected, but clean-shaven. Like most Sokorans, he had blue eyes, but his hair was darker, almost brown instead of blonde. He had the look of a laborer, possibly a woodcutter, judging by the axe hanging from his belt.

The man walked up, pulling his hood off and sat down. "Ranger Joryd?" he asked.

Leif nodded. "I am. I was told you had a contract?"

"That I do. It's a simple contract, though I know the payment is lower than the usual fare," he said.

"Why not take this up with Huntsman Eirik? Grunier is part of his governance."

The sound of chairs scuffing the floor behind him drew his attention. Leif turned his head, glimpsing the Blades from the corner of his eye. They were listening in.

The man swallowed hard and leaned in closer. "There have been rising tensions," he whispered. "I know some of you take contracts, regardless of governance. I thought it best not to involve the Rangers here and ask for outside help."

Leif narrowed his eyes and leaned forward. "What sort of tensions, Sig?"

"Thran Agrim has been assigning contracts from the boards to his men and the Blades," Sig replied. "He had been voicing his dislike for your autonomy for months. Your Huntsman is furious and nearly come to blows with him over the matter."

Leif curled his lip. A Thran giving out contracts violated the treaty. "What of his daughter? Doesn't she handle the day-to-day affairs and contract assignments?"

"She has abandoned the Rangers and joined the Blades..." he answered. "I've word that she said something about a new future for Sokoras."

Leif blinked and stared at the man. How could Ylva do that?

"How interesting, Leif," Talyn chimed in. "I thought all of you were *family*?"

He tensed. Talyn had never spoken in public before. Sig, however, had appeared not to have heard him. "This contract, tell me about it."

"People have gone missing," Sig said. "In the past, these things happen. Sometimes a Blade got too drunk and well... you can imagine the rest. The frequency is growing and I fear it is far worse than the Blades."

"How does this concern you, Sig?"

"Because my daughter was one of them," he said. "No one has seen her in days."

Talyn sighed. "How boring," he said. "I was hoping it would be something more entertaining."

Leif bit his lip. "How old is she?"

"Fifteen winters," he replied. "She was to be betrothed to a local trader's son upon reaching her sixteenth year. The boy is distraught and is the reason I have the funds to make the contract."

"You don't suppose he's responsible?"

Sig shook his head. "No, Dennig is a good lad, and he loves my daughter very much."

"What was her name?"

"Brenja," he said.

Leif drew his lip taut, fighting to keep his emotions in check. Sig's eyes were showing how hard this was for him. "Keep your shards."

"Leif! Are you daft?!" Talyn commented.

Leif gripped the handle of his mug. *It's nice to see what you care about, raven,* he thought.

"Ranger, I can't do that," Sig said. "I know the rules. Not taking payment will violate your oaths."

"Barter then," Leif replied. "In exchange for searching, I want you to keep Eirik informed of anything that could be a threat to the Rangers. Tell the son that he is to do the same."

Sig smiled, his eyes watering. "You're a good man, Ranger Joryd."

"I think you give me too much credit."

Sig shook his head. "I don't think the Rangers get enough." He reached into his belt pouch and pulled out a silver barrette. "Denneg gave this to Brenja as a gift. I hear you can find people if you have something that belongs to them."

Leif took the barrette, thumbing it between his fingers, then pocketed it in the pouch on his belt. Dennig must be wealthy to give such an elaborate gift.

Sig stood, "I pray your hunt is bountiful," he said, sounding hopeful and giving a polite nod. The woodcutter glanced at the Blades. They were still watching. Ignoring them, he exited into the foyer, then stepped outside.

Talyn flew down from his perch, his attention still drawn to the Blades. "So we took a boring job," he grumbled. "I was hoping for a real bounty."

Leif rolled his eyes and took another drink. "We're leaving."

Talyn quickly hopped on his shoulder. "Into the barren cold we go…" he mumbled softly.

"If you hate it so much, then be a snow leopard," Leif replied. "After three months, you still complain when you have the power to do something about it."

He stepped out the front door, the cold greeting him along with the sound of a dejected sigh. *Keeper take you, bird, I swear.*

"I can't help that I have my preferences, even if ravens are adept at handling the cold," Talyn replied.

Leif paused. "What?!" He didn't have to look to get a sense that Talyn was grinning to himself. "You mean, when I had to tuck you away and carry you for eight miles in that storm because you were worried about freezing to death, you would have been fine?"

Talyn playfully nuzzled his cheek. "You were so warm," he replied.

"I swear, I should cook you."

Talyn scoffed. "As if you could," he said. "Besides, I'm a tough old bird. You'd only choke."

Leif sighed, gripping the hilt of his short swords. "I have only myself to blame for this."

Talyn cawed softly. "Ironic isn't it?"

Leif shook his head and stepped toward the nearest alleyway. He took the barrette from his belt pouch and closed his eyes. Soaking in the feel of its silver craftsmanship and hairpiece's teeth as he brushed his fingers against it, the Ranger called upon his powers. If the girl was alive, there would be a connection, a Thread, as his brothers called it, tying her to the barrette.

It was a skill known as Finding. Something the Skegs taught, but only to those who survived the tests and had committed themselves to the Rangers. Level of mastery varied, but those with true talent could follow a Thread for miles.

"You're using *it*, aren't you, Leif?" He sounded so excited, as if it never got old. "You must explain how this works. I have never heard of magic like this."

Magic, huh? I suppose it is...

Leif continued to feel the barrette, the cold nipping his fingers. The Thread was faint, strained and ready to snap. The girl was alive, though barely.

"Yew!"

A bright flash flared across his vision. Leif fell forward, eyes fluttering open. Through the haze, he recognized the Blades from the Grey Beard. They were still drunk, their gait holding a swagger as they drew their weapons. Two had skeggox, while the third a skiirg, a type of longsword.

Talyn... you could have warned me.

"We saw yew talkin' with that local. Yew don't belong in Grunier, ya flag is differnt."

"Oh look, Leif, it's a rare breed of human known as a moron," Talyn commented. "Actually, it's the worst kind, a drunken moron."

Despite the throbbing pain in his skull. Leif cracked a smile and rolled onto his back. Talyn had his moments, few as they were. "I wasn't aware my flag was unwelcome here," he grunted.

As a general rule, Rangers visiting a different governance were required to wear the flag of their Hunstman some place visible. Some had them tattooed. It was a matter of courtesy. Shuet's flag was a blue standard with a warhammer in front of a bushel of White Fern.

One of them sneered. "Yew Rangers trounce about, like kings. That'll change soon nough'. We'll be takin's ya jobs."

Leif put the barrette away and held his hands up. The haze was clearing. "Look, I took my contract and I'll leave. It doesn't require me having to return."

"I don't think yew understands, Ranga," the one with the skiirg said. "You 'ave to pay a penalty for settin' foot in our town."

Killing them would be easy. They were drunk and overconfident. It wasn't an option, though, and would only cause more problems for Eirik. Bodvar was known for being vengeful about his losses.

The trio moved in, encircling him. Cautiously, Leif pulled himself up, keeping an eye on them. The Blade armed with the skiirg came in, slashing at his back. Leif turned, clutching his hands around the Blade's wrist and twisting it.

The man screamed, dropping the weapon, but his fellows were quick to step in. They swung their skeggox and Leif stepped back, twisting their companion's wrist further and pulling the Blade's arm behind his back. The man screamed again from the motion, an audible pop sounding.

The pair missed, and he released the third, pushing him into his friends. They dodged, letting him fall onto the stone of the snow-covered alley while he cried about his wounded arm. Undeterred, they swung again, each rotating in rhythm. By their movements, they were used to fighting together. Each was careful not to let the other get in the way.

Leif glanced behind him. The dead-end at the end of the alley was fast approaching. He had to fight to keep from drawing his short swords. Even drunk, the pair were skilled, but he knew he was better.

With the wall getting closer, the aim of the two Blades was becoming more accurate. Adrenaline was sobering them up. Their patterns were growing predictable and Leif, stepping in, caught the Blade to his right under the arm with a quick jab.

The man stumbled, grunting, and nearly dropping his skeggox. His partner came in attempting to seize the opportunity, but Leif cut him across the jaw with his right fist. He shuffled back, taken off guard, and Leif followed up with a left hook, sending him tumbling on to the stone.

He turned to the other, just catching sight of the third Blade as he barreled into him. The man's shoulder collided with his abdomen, knocking the breath out of him, and they went tumbling deeper into the alley.

Another flash blitzed Leif's vision as he hit the side of his head against the stone wall at the end of the alley. He rolled onto his back, shaking his head when he felt a hard blow to his stomach, then another to the face.

"Yew, scrivving bastard!" one Blade shouted. "Yew wrecked ma arm!"

The beating continued; the haze unrelenting. Leif faintly heard the other two laughing as they kicked his back and sides. *Talyn... why do you only watch?*

Desperately, Leif lashed out, his fist like a hammer. A high-pitched squeal followed and through the stone, the faint vibration of something toppling. "He it' ma scroat!" one of them screamed. "Kill em!"

"Now, now, boys," Talyn said. "That's just not polite. You can beat him, but you can't kill him. He's *mine*!"

His voice was deeper, more baritone. There was power in it, like one who carries authority. Like one who should be feared. A scream followed and behind it, Leif felt something wet splash onto his face. He turned, pain wracking body, and shook his head, trying to clear the fog.

It hadn't been a singular scream. All three of them were screaming. Something large was tearing them apart. He could hear bestial roars between the screams, like an ice bear or a dragon. A dragon, though, couldn't fit in the alley.

When the fog in his mind cleared, Leif saw Talyn, in the form of a raven, his feathers soaked in the Blade's blood. The carnage was horrific. What little of them remained was half-eaten. The width of the bite on one Blade's torso was as large as a man's head.

Talyn simply stood there, a feral glint in his black eyes. "I really did hate them," he said. "Their thoughts were so distracting in the inn. Like an inane buzzing that wouldn't stop." He sighed, shaking his head. "Well, no loss. We just have to clean this up and move on. You have a contract, after all."

"Talyn, won't someone hear?"

The raven was getting easier to read. There was a feeling that he was smiling. "No one heard anything, Leif."

***

He was an interesting creature. Resilient too. One would have thought his injuries would have been more severe. Thankfully, Leif was so strong. Using magic to keep him going would have been less than ideal.

Talyn sighed happily. These past few months had been full of entertainment. Still, Yggsid had yet to be their destination. The druid grove was always the goal.

Leif had purchased a horse a month ago. Well, bartered for it. The beasts were absurdly expensive. Watching the measures needed to maintain it was interesting.

The creature was a monster, like a mountain of muscle, with thick hair covering its hooves. The barding Leif acquired to keep it warm was well crafted. But with what it would have cost him in shards, it made sense why most Sokorans used yaks over horses.

The horse made a statement, though. People took notice and showed him a bit more respect when they saw him riding it. It was doubtful it had been Leif's intent. He wasn't that kind of human.

"Leif, why did you buy this thing?"

"Because I got the feeling we'd be traveling to a lot of out of the way places. Binyorn horses can travel far and carry a lot. Plus, I'm not walking across the breadth of Sokoras at your leisure."

Talyn grinned inwardly. *Practical.*

"I need to ask you," he said. "How is it I am starting to get an idea of what you are feeling?"

Talyn paused. This was unexpected.

"Talyn?" he pressed.

"It seems we have become connected..."

"You don't sound happy about that," he commented.

"Well, I would rather keep my feelings to myself."

Leif laughed. "You selfish feather duster! You think it well and good to know everything about everyone else, but when it comes to you, no one should know anything."

"See you get it, Leif. This is why we make such a good team."

A wry smile etched its way onto his face. "Team? Is that what this is?" he asked. "I thought I was playing poor jailer to a creature I cannot understand."

"Jailer?!" Talyn replied. "Leif, I'm wounded," he added, nuzzling up against the Ranger's cheek. "I thought we shared something special?"

Leif curled his lip, drawing it taut. "I really don't like you..."

"Aww, Leif, is that what you say to someone who saved your life?"

The ranger's expression changed, eyes growing distant. Talyn stared at him. Strangely, though, Leif's mind had become clouded and hard to read. *Perhaps it was too soon to change. There were other ways I could have dealt with them.*

"Leif, where are we going?"

"Viktor has Fern plantations scattered throughout his territory. The larger ones are marked on the most current regional maps. I get the feeling we'll find the girl at one of them. Rauld isn't far. It's the largest and has developed into a small town."

"This Fern, what is it?" But at the mention of the plant, Talyn noted Leif appeared annoyed.

"Medicine, narcotic, or poison, take your pick," Leif answered. "When properly refined, it can help ease pain, or keep you warm."

"And if improperly refined?"

"It wrecks the body," he replied. "The more you take, the more you need to keep warm. Eventually, you freeze to death. Fern addicts are violent and dangerous without their fix."

*How curious...*Talyn thought. "Does this Viktor sell it as a drug?"

Leif's expression hardened. "He used to, so they say, before he became Thran. He sold it to the Dark Guilds of Absion."

"Typical human," Talyn commented. "He used the money to raise an army and become a king."

"You sound like you've seen that plenty of times, Talyn."

More than you know, human. They were all the same, each scrambling for power, prestige, or position. Like ants, each clamored to be at the top of the pile until another knocked them over. When would they learn how useless such ambitions were?

"Talyn?" Leif asked. "You're brooding."

Talyn narrowed his eyes. "This is going to get irritating quickly."

Leif laughed. "I think it's my turn to get some enjoyment out of our arrangement."

Talyn turned his head, pecking him on the side of the head. "Quiet you! Or I'll make you dance like a marionette on strings."

Leif reached over, swatting at him. "Talyn!"

Talyn took flight, gliding toward the horse's head, and using it for a perch. The Ranger's expression was mixed, somewhere between annoyance and showing that he felt as if he had won a minor victory. He pivoted, facing forward, catching sight of something poking through the treeline.

"Rauld, I take it?" he asked, looking over his shoulder.

Leif nodded. "Rauld."

***

Leif cringed as he examined its walls. Rauld looked more like an elaborate prison, its iron gates uninviting. They weren't high but were sturdy and made of stone. Viktor's Bears patrolled the walls, their watchful eyes shifting between the street and the world outside.

"I don't like the atmosphere or those men," Talyn commented.

"Are you going to eat them too?"

Talyn cawed. "No," he replied snidely. "They probably taste as horrible as the other three."

Leif rolled his eyes. *You amaze me sometimes.*

Leif rode in past the iron gates. After laying eyes on the village, the heaviness he felt outside the walls grew. The buildings were organized and streets easy to navigate. The uniformity was unsettling.

Leif studied the guards patrolling the streets, then eyed the people going about their business. "Talyn, find me the name of an inn, please."

Surprisingly, he took off without complaint, moving between buildings and vanishing from view.

"You there!"

Leif turned to his right. A trio of Bears were staring him down. They carried bucklers and had skeggox hanging from their belts.

"What's your business here, *Ranger*," the one in the lead asked.

"Just a simple contract," Leif replied, reaching into his belt pouch and pulling the barrette out. "I'm supposed to deliver this."

The Bear narrowed his eyes, his brow furrowed with suspicion. "Seems like strange that a Ranger would deliver such a thing to a place like this in leu of a courier."

"Name one courier that would want to make the trip," Leif replied. "Especially with the recent weather." As if on cue, a cold gust a wind whipped through the gate.

The Bear narrowed his eyes, grinding his teeth. "Where are you stay-ing, *Ranger*?"

"The Sheep's Den," Talyn chimed in, landing atop the horse's head.

A wave of relief washed over him. Talyn's timing couldn't have been better. "The Sheep's Den, I'll only be here for a couple of days to resupply and I'll be on my way."

The Bear leaned back, whispering something among the other two. Both men nodded. "You have two days. If you don't leave by then, we'll throw you out *without* your horse."

"As you wish."

They stepped away, but even as he passed, Leif felt their eyes on his back.

"Clever Leif," Talyn commented. "You surprise me."

"Should I take that as a compliment?"

Talyn cawed. "Yes. It means you aren't stupid."

Leif frowned. *When you say it that way, it still sounds condescending.*

"You know they're going to watch you, right?" Talyn commented.

"I would be surprised if they didn't. I'm starting to think Viktor is up to something."

Talyn bobbed his head. "I would be shocked if he wasn't."

***

The Sheep's Den was a suitable cover, after all. Though it seemed that Talyn played some part in that. The main room was open and spacious. There were other travelers here, too. Some of them merchants. The stable had been big enough for Slep, though the innkeeper insisted on charging more shards that it was worth to keep the horse under its roof.

So far, Viktor's men had kept their distance and Talyn hadn't commented about anyone watching them. Either they didn't care or were being especially cautious. Either way, the snowfall had resumed and was heavier than before.

Talyn had resumed his normal perch on Leif's shoulder, his gaze fixed on the streets and Rauld's people. He was acting strangely interested. Perhaps it was the way the Bears were behaving or how inhospitable the village felt. Still, there wasn't enough distance or time for him to return before they had asked about an inn.

"You already knew, didn't you?"

"Knew what?" Talyn replied.

"You knew about this place and the inn, even before you understood my intent."

A soft gust of wind blew through the street. The silence was telling. *So, you have been flying around on your own while I sleep.*

Leif sighed, shifting his attention to the street. He touched the barrette, following the weak thread he sensed connecting it to Sig's daughter. After a few minutes, he stopped, casually stepping close to a nearby building and leaning against it.

A large wooden wall blocked his path. No doubt the plantation's fields were on the other side. They built ramparts into it and along their paths were more of Viktor's Bears keeping watch. None of this felt right, but the Thread led past the wall.

"She's in there, isn't she?" Talyn asked.

Leif pursed his lip. "It appears so."

Talyn sighed. "Then Viktor is enslaving his people to work the fields," he said. "How typical."

"I guess warlords are creatures of habit."

"Oh, Leif, you have no idea," he replied wryly.

His age was showing again. You could hear it in his tone. It was like listening to a jaded old man who had seen a lot of terrible things.

"So wait till nightfall?" Talyn asked.

"We do. While we wait, we had best shop for supplies."

"Appearances are important," Talyn chided. "We can't have others interfering."

Leif tried to crack a smile. "Well, you could always eat them."

Talyn hissed softly. "Leif, I don't think I'll be helping you again any-time soon!"

Leif sighed. *Why do I feel your help only involves killing people?*

***

The chill of the night air was unusually bitter. Leif felt it seeping in through his furs and armor. Oddly, Talyn had taken the form of snow leopard, but his behavior was different. He was more cautious. His muscles were tensed and ears were twitching back and forth.

"What are you staring at?" he whispered.

Leif grinned, adjusting the rope and hook hanging on his shoulder, and shook his head. *They can see you in this form, can't they?*

With Talyn following close behind, Leif stalked closer to the planta-tion's main gate. Four guards were patrolling along the rampart and two more stood on either side of the gate. The wall itself was about fifteen feet.

"We're not going to assault that, are we?" Talyn asked.

"No, I just wanted to see how heavy the guard was in case we had to fight our way out."

"Good, because I wasn't going to help you."

Leif sighed. *You pick now, to pout like a child.*

Using the buildings for cover, he kept watch on the patrols while moving along the wall's perimeter. Talyn remained ever close and eerily silent. After several minutes of waiting, Leif noticed a window. Leif stepped out when Talyn abruptly locked his jaws around his ankle and tugged.

"Patrol," he whispered.

Leif flattened himself against the building, the faint sound of two men laughing, reaching his ears. Minutes later, two Bears passed by. Leif kept his eyes on their backs until they turned the corner. He shifted his attention back to the wall. Their window was gone.

"We could always tell Sig she's dead," Talyn offered. "Chances are she is."

"No, she's alive."

"How do you know?" Talyn's tone showed his curiosity.

"Because I do."

He simply shrugged, at least that's how it appeared, and crept forward, his attention on the wall. After a few minutes, he spoke up.

"We should move now."

Leif stepped forward. The guards were far enough out. He rushed to the wall, quickly taking the rope and hooked it over. To his surprise, the grapple made no sound when it found purchase.

He scowled, pulling himself up. *Not helping, he says! So infuriating!*

Talyn scaled the wall with relative ease and Leif unhooked the rope upon reaching the top of the rampart. He climbed over, taking the grapple to the opposite side and anchoring it, he rappelled down. Once at the base of the wall, Talyn took the hook in his mouth and tossed over, then leapt, landing on his feet.

"Bears!" he snapped harshly.

Leaf bundled the rope and flattened himself against the wall. The footsteps of the guards on the rampart grew louder. Silently he prayed that under the cover of night, and in the dim torchlight, they wouldn't notice the drag marks of the rope or his footprints in the snow. Once their footsteps drifted away, he and Talyn sprinted through the fields, using the large bushels of fern for cover.

The main hall was enormous, its stone structure reminiscent of a keep. Based on the scattered assortment of windows, it had three levels. To the right of the hall was a set of smaller buildings. The fern was likely processed there before they took it to the storehouse beyond them.

Leif stared at the hall. The Thread was strongest here. The quiet pricked the hairs on his neck. Something wasn't right. There were no guards.

"Talyn, do you hear anything?" he whispered.

Talyn shook his head. "Nothing." He stalked closer, keeping low to the ground, then turned his head toward a smaller building several yards off to the left of the hall. His ears twitched.

"Viktor's Bears are there."

Leif sized up the building. It was probably large enough to house twenty or so. *Why are they not on patrol?*

It was hard to tell if Talyn was reading his mind, but without a word, the shapeshifter stretched out, his fur turning black, while muscle and bone reshaped themselves. Once the transformation was complete, he took the air and began checking the windows.

After finishing with the upper floors, he stopped and flew back. "It would seem that the workers are being kept on pallets and crammed into rooms together."

"How many?"

"Fifty workers per room at least," he replied.

Leif locked his jaw and crept closer to the hall. Talyn shifted forms, becoming a snow leopard and followed. They stuck close to the hall's perimeter, stopping at its main doors. Leif tested them and they gave, cracking opening.

"Strange. Shouldn't they be barred so late at night?" Talyn asked.

He wasn't wrong. "They should. No one simply leaves their front door unbarred or unlocked."

Leif fought back his surprise as Talyn moved ahead, slipping between the cracks in the double doors. It felt somehow off that he wasn't the one going in first.

A soft chuff escaped the shapeshifter's throat. "I'm just curious," he muttered, then added, "this is no longer boring."

Leif shook his head and followed him. *I doubt I'll ever understand you...*

The hall was like any other. Rows of tables and chairs were lined up neatly along its length, with an avenue between them leading to a platform and a table at the far end. The master of the house and his chosen circle or family would sit here. At the center of the avenue was a grand firepit whose embers had long died out.

Above the firepit hung a smokestack with chambers branching out from along the ceiling. It was almost like looking at a stone tree with a break at the base of the trunk. The 'branches' of the stack likely connected with rooms on the other floors to keep them warm. With the embers died out, it was apparent that the guards watching the workers had little regard for them or any interest in making sure they stayed warm.

Three sets of doors sat on either side of the hall and two more beyond the platform itself. It was likely the two doors at the end led to the kitchens, pantries, and food stores. Their doors on either side would lead to the hall's sleeping chambers and guest rooms.

Talyn paused, turning his head left, then right. "This way," he whispered, heading left.

"How do you know?"

"Because I memorized the layout when I checked the windows," he replied, sounding a bit irritated. "Just accept I'm smarter than you, Leif."

Leif scowled. "I should make a pelt out of you..."

Talyn softly purred and simply walked away. "You can try," he replied.

He followed the shapeshifter toward the middle door on the left. Talyn sat on his hind legs, balanced himself and pawed the door handle. The door eased open, and he pushed his way through.

"Seems you've had practice," Leif commented.

"I'm still not telling you how old I am, Leif."

Leif cracked a grin and followed him in. "It was worth a try."

The spiral staircase looked as if it extended between each floor. It was steep and, like the rest of the hall, made of stone. Leif reached into his pouch and thumbed the barrette between his fingers. Brenja was close.

"Your turn," Talyn said.

Taking the lead, he followed the stairs to a small landing on the second floor and checked the door. Like the doors in the main hall, it wasn't locked. Opening the door, Leif focused his attention on there the Thread was pulling him. Brenja's connection to the barrette was strongest down the hall to his right. He paused, noting the torches sitting in their cradles had burned out.

"So you finally noticed," Talyn commented.

"Talyn... what is this?"

The shapeshifter cracked a feral smile. "Consider it a perk of our arrangement," he replied. "You've been too consumed with your work to notice these past three months."

Leif took a breath, steadying himself. He knew he couldn't lose focus now. Answers come later. *So now I can see in the dark...*

He followed the hall to the door where the pull was the strongest and opened it. The barrette slipped from his fingers as he stared into the room in stunned silence. True to Talyn's report, there were fifty workers all laid out on palettes. What he hadn't said was that they were emaciated and half-starved.

Pulling himself together, Leif scooped up the barrette and quietly slinked into the room. The workers were asleep, some of them snoring. Against the wall hung the furs and clothing they were expected to wear while working the fields. White Fern was an unusual plant. It thrived in the winter but struggled in the summer months.

Leif reached the window. Brenja's thread was pulsing, and he turned to see a young girl close to the same state as the others. She had blond, stringy hair and pale skin. Her appearance was reminiscent of a Fern addict. Her arms and body were more defined, and with the simple shift she wore, it was hard not to notice how beautiful she was.

He knelt, slipping between her and her neighbor's pallet. *"Brenja..."* Brenja stirred, rolling onto her side. She was shivering. Leif pulled her blanket over her. *"Brenja."*

Her eyes slowly opened, but they were distant, as if seeing past him. "It is time to work?" she asked. "Viktor will be happy. The fern is growing well."

Talyn growled softly. "Kill her," he said coldly. "She is dead. I know this magic. This alchemy."

"Kill me?" she asked. "Is Viktor displeased? I'll work harder. Do better. I want to make him happy. He deserves our devotion."

Leif reached for the wall, steadying himself. He gagged, fighting back the bile in his throat. "Talyn... what is this?!"

"Old knowledge, very old. It enslaves the mind," he replied. "I know this plant you call White Fern now. I will not speak its name, but I know it."

There was no mirth in his voice, no cynicism. Only disgust and anger. His expression said the sight of her and the others had dredged up an ancient memory.

"Kill her, Leif, it's the kindest thing you can do. Sig doesn't have to know."

"No, Talyn, we can take her to Yggsid. The druids can help her!"

He crept closer, his yellow eyes turning black. "Are they Aetharian?" he asked, his voice growing deeper in tone. "Are they keepers of ancient lore? No... the cure for her is gone. She will die soon. Whatever this Viktor is attempting, it is clear he does not understand the alchemy." Leif stared into his eyes. It felt as if the inky blackness within those orbs would consume him. "Kill her... Or I will."

"No," she said, raising her voice. "I'll be good. I'll work harder! Please!"

"Shhh," Leif whispered. "No one is going to hurt you. Your father sent me to find you."

"No," she replied. "I am home. This is my home. Viktor asked me to stay to help him. We're going to make a future for Sokoras."

Leif blinked, his eyes opening wide. "What did you say?"

"We're going to create a future in Sokoras," she repeated. "Viktor will be High Thran."

Leif shifted his weight, leaning harder on the wall and covered his mouth. He took slow breaths, fighting to keep from throwing up. It suddenly made sense why Ylva had turned her back on the Rangers... If Eirik finds out.

Talyn growled. "Leif."

"You look sick," she said. "Do you want me to make you feel better?"

Leif shook his head, her words barely registering. He felt someone touch his face, then press their lips to his, followed by their tongue. At that moment, the present snapped back into place and he grabbed Brenja, pushing her against the wall.

"What are you doing?!"

"Leif! Your voice!" Talyn said.

"Making you feel better," she said. "The guards say I'm good at that."

Leif stood, using the wall as an anchor. "Go to sleep, Brenja. It will make Viktor happy," he whispered.

Like a child, Brenja smiled happily, though she was still shivering. She laid down, pulling the heavy blanket over herself, and closed her eyes. Leif turned to the rest of the room, his heart pounding, and drew his short swords.

"Just her, Leif," Talyn said. "Just her. They can be replaced. She is the contract."

Leif looked at her. It was so unfair. She would have had a life, a chance to have a family, but Viktor had taken that. He knelt beside her, his short sword shaking in his hand. "Lie still," he whispered. "Keep your eyes closed."

Brenja smiled. "Okay," she replied. It was like talking to a child. So innocent and trusting.

Leif sheathed the short sword, then placed his left hand over Brenja's mouth and clamped her nose shut with his fingers. Because of whatever she had been given, Brenja never opened her eyes while trying to fight him off. In her partially emaciate state, she was too weak and soon went limp. He pulled his hand away, a wave of guilt washing over him.

"She was already dead, Leif," Talyn whispered.

"It still feels like murder," he replied.

The shapeshifter sighed. "Moral semantics, Leif."

"Shut up, Talyn." Leif sheathed his other short sword and taking Brenja's body in his arms, he started toward the door.

"Where are you taking that?" Talyn asked.

Leif clutched her close and turned back to him. "To the firepit downstairs. We need to burn her body before sunrise."

***

Leif was quiet, his eyes empty and expression plain as the surrounding snow. Since rising at dawn, no amount of jabbing or insult had roused him to speech. The Ranger simply stared at the horizon toward Grunier. Only the dull sound of Slep's hooves clomping in the snow, and the occasional snort he often did, broke the monotony.

Burning the human girl's body hadn't been enough. Too much evidence remained of their presence. Magic had been the only recourse. Talyn glanced back at the Ranger. Leif made no comment about invoking magic or the intensity of the conjured flames. His expression was, as it is now, making it hard to know if he had been furious or relieved. His mind was still clouded and hard to read.

This is all boring. I should have been the one to kill her. He's being ridiculous.

"Talyn," he said. "I need a favor."

Talyn froze, tilting his head curiously. "A favor?"

"I want you to become a snow owl and deliver a message to Eirik in Grunier," he said. "Then I need you to deliver a second message to Sig."

"Leif, you know I don't speak to others." Talyn narrowed his eyes. *Why is he assuming I can take such a form?*

"While you slept, I wrote the letters, and sealed them," Leif replied stoically. "I will make camp outside of Grunier and wait for your return."

Talyn stretched his wings, studying him. "If I were inclined to do this," he said. "Then I want to go to Yggsid."

Leif shifted his eyes from the horizon. "You will do this," he said, tugging on Slep's reigns, bringing the horse to a halt. "Or we will not move from this spot."

His tone was flat and empty. Leif had meant every word and inwardly Talyn seethed before letting the moment pass and finally sighing. "Fine, I will deliver these. Then we go to Yggsid."

Chapter Three

Talyn eyed the bleak winter landscape, his thoughts drifting. *It's almost time.* He turned his head, studying Lief from over his shoulder. He wasn't saying much, but for now, it was best not to push him. The ranger needed to simmer, allowing his thoughts to carry them on whatever wind was appropriate.

I wonder what you will think of the world beyond this wretched wasteland?

Talyn closed his eyes, drawing upon his power. As always, nausea wasn't far behind. The connection was faint, but the power he sensed was coming from Ygsidd. What at first had been a venture of curiosity to see the ancient grove had now become something more purposeful.

Slep shook his head, shaking the snow from his mane and interrupting the raven's concentration. The shapeshifter sighed, steadying himself, as he clutched the horse's mane in his talons. *Stupid animal.*

Talyn lifted his eyes to the sky, smirking to himself at how much the stars had changed as time over the long centuries. Save for a handful, most mortal simpletons were clueless about the scope of things. If they were to learn, most might simply roll over and die.

"You still haven't asked me, Lief," he said.

"Asked you what, Talyn?" he asked.

"It's been days now and as per your usual rounds, you have been wandering from village to village on our roundabout way to Yggsid. Yet in all that time, since discovering it in Rauld, you never once asked me how it is you can see in the dark."

He sighed, apathy written all over his face. "Does it matter? Because of you, I can see in the dark. It's that simple, and it's useful."

Talyn tightened his grip on Slep's mane. *Useful, he says!*

"Why are you so angry?" Lief asked. "Are you wanting to play another game?"

Talyn shook his head. "No, I just wanted to talk."

"Then talk, bird," Leif replied. "I'll just listen. It seems that's all you want, anyway."

Talyn stared at him. "You were right," he said. "I was lonely."

Lief narrowed his eyes, his suspicion showing and pulling back on Slep's reins. "What is this?"

"This is me answering your questions," Talyn replied. "What do you think it is?"

"A ploy, or a trick, maybe something you do for your own amusement?" he said. "You lie or say enough to sound convincing. You do this as easily as a man breathes."

"Wouldn't you after so many years on your own?" Talyn asked. "Being alone changes you, Leif."

Leif leaned forward in the saddle, distrust showing in his eyes. "How long have you been alone, Talyn?" His was tone flat and empty. It was obvious he expected some embellished answer or flowery response.

"Since The Fall," Talyn answered. "Around the time when Dakren's hold on this world shattered under the weight of their ambitions."

Leif leaned back in the saddle and shook his head. "How is that possible?" he asked. "That would make you..."

"Ancient, by your standards, or two to three full Shaylin lifetimes, by elven measurement," Talyn commented. "Though that may be inaccurate."

Leif grew quiet; his expression, reflective. It was interesting to see his reaction. All suspicion had vanished. He'd even relaxed his shoulders.

"What are you Talyn?" he abruptly asked.

Inwardly, Talyn smirked. "Something that should not be." He tensed up again, his expression souring. Leif was about to close himself off. "Did you know magic has rules? That it follows a strict 'code' as it were."

"I've heard the druids speak of The Cycle," Leif replied.

Talyn sighed, shook his head, then turned to the smattering of trees a few yards away. "Take me there," he ordered.

Lief frowned, but reluctantly agreed, tugging on Slep's reins and urging him toward the pines. Talyn hopped off once they were close enough, then transformed into a snow leopard. He stalked closer to one of the pines and leaned back on his hind legs, resting his front paws on its trunk.

"This will do. Go ahead and dismount, Leif, then draw one of your swords."

Lief dismounted and drew one of his swords. He appeared curious, but skeptical.

"Hit the tree," Talyn said. "Hit it as often as you like."

Talyn stood back and Lief struck the tree, but after the first strike, it was like something inside snapped, and he didn't stop. The ranger kept striking it over and over until at last, the shortblade fell from his grasp, and he cried out at the top of his lungs, banging his fist against it. Lief fell to his knees, tears in his eyes and on his cheeks.

Talyn crept closer. "Feel better?"

Leif rested his forehead against the pine tree and shook his head. "It's not fair, you know," he said. "Brenja could have had so much more."

"Everyone has the opportunity to become something, Lief. To have more." Talyn replied. "But not everyone gets the chance to seize it."

"So you simply let them die or end their lives?"

"Mercy comes in many forms, Lief, and death is most often the kindest thing you can offer anyone," Talyn answered. "Life is often a torturous prison. For some, it's a punishment."

"Is that what you think?" Leif asked. "That your longevity is a prison?"

"I think my existence serves as an example to foolish mortals who desire to bend or break the rules."

The ranger's curiosity piqued. Even with bloodshot eyes, you could see it. "What are you Talyn?"

"You see this pine," Talyn replied. "Before you struck it, it was whole and complete. Now, after you maimed it, with the sap bleeding through in places, it has scars."

"So what you're telling me is that you result from this scarring or bleeding?"

"Simply put, yes, and not of my own will," Talyn said.

"So during the game, which story was true?" Leif asked.

Talyn grinned, his incisors showing. "Perhaps one of them was true, or perhaps all of them were lies..."

"Or perhaps a bit of the truth was hidden in each one," Leif countered.

Talyn let a feral grin slip. "Perhaps indeed, Lief. You see, this is why I like you so much."

His face broke into a partial frown. "You're still dancing around the full answer."

"Maybe, but you know more now than you did before." The answer didn't appear very satisfying to the ranger. But at least, judging by his expression, Leif was less melancholy.

"It really was too much to hope for," he said.

Talyn grinned. "Some answers, Leif, aren't as obscure as you think."

***

Leif regarded him quizzically, then turned to the tree. By his own admission, Talyn may have been right. It felt like a large part of the answer was here. He touched the gash marks with his left hand. He could feel them through the rough leather of his gloves.

What he was before is not what is he now...

Of all the misdirections Talyn had spoken and words he had offered, perhaps this was the largest part of the puzzle after all. He had let it slip that he was old on several occasions, pretended to rant or show perceived anger. In the end, it was hard to know what was an act, and what was the truth. Still, his slight smile over the comment about bits of the truth being revealed spoke volumes.

You little bastard.

"Leif, why are you smiling?" Talyn asked.

Lief grabbed his shortblade and sheathed it. "Because lonely people do curious things, Talyn."

Talyn nodded. "They do, don't they?" he replied with a slight grin. "So you have you found your answer?"

"Perhaps I have, but time will tell."

Talyn smirked. "You sound like me," he purred.

"It's hard not to with you prattling on in my ears," Leif commented.

Talyn shifted, then resumed his perch on top of Slep's head. "Leif, it just dawned on me," he said. "I haven't asked how old you are. It's hard to tell with you humans unless you show gray in your hair."

Leif grinned. "I'm ten percent of twice that of a young Shaylin who is considered a full-fledged adult in winters, plus five."

Talyn narrowed his eyes. "You've been paying too much attention, Leif," he grumbled.

"I had a good teacher of intrigue and wordplay."

"I'll have to reprimand this teacher of yours for his carelessness."

He was trying to veil it in his tone, but Talyn was amused. Leif smiled and shook his head, mounted Slep and reined him toward Ygsidd.

I suppose that in time I will get a better grasp of the Kings Board. For now, I'll take what victories I can garner.

***

"You're twenty-five winters," Talyn blurted out at the village gate.

Lief grinned. "Maybe," he said, dismounting and walking past the gate with Slep in tow. "Or maybe I'm older."

Talyn narrowed his eyes. *He's smarter than I gave him credit for. Either way, the math doesn't lie.* "What are we doing here, Leif?"

"Alif is the last stop before Yggsid," he replied. "It's my job to take contracts and report in to Huntsman Shuet. I have no reason to be at Yggsid, especially since it's part of Huntsman Wulf's governance."

"So you're taking contracts along to way to show that you are fulfilling your duties."

"It's more than that," he replied. "I don't have permissions who wander as I please, not without a contract. I get my contracts directly from Huntsman Shuet and his Skegs."

"So all these stops you've been making are under pretense?"

"More or less," he replied. "Small villages don't always have the means to afford us, so aiding them for free or reaching an amicable agreement helps both parties. Free lodging and food for a ranger passing through is typical fare, but not longer than for two days."

Smart indeed. The Sokoran Rangers were interesting and are more organized than it appeared. It was likely they were a linchpin, keeping some semblance of order in this cursed land.

"So you're telling your Huntsman that you are making rounds in the outlying areas because they are so often overlooked?"

"Essentially," Leif replied. "I can't go further than Yggsid however, only Huntsman Wulf and Eirik's Rangers are allowed near Savar's territory. Huntsman Shuet hates the man."

"So he refuses the help Savar's people out of some personal grudge?"

Lief winced. "More like he prefers letting Eirik or Wulf deal with such a difficult man. Eirik especially, most of the Thran are afraid of him."

The politics were interesting. The Rangers were very similar to the Knights of the Shield in Baneese. Regardless of the barons' borders, the knights exist to protect the people. However, they had to adhere to the laws of each region. "So whose governance lies where?"

"Huntsman Shuet handles the town of Svaren, plus Illhiem's and Grenden's territories. Huntsman Wulf is in charge of contracts in the eastern territories along the border controlled by Dag, Thulm, and Henrik. Henrik rarely asks for aid, however. Yggsid is also Wulf's responsibility because of his wife. I hear she is a force to be reckoned with."

"Eirik handles Viktor, Savar and Jormund's territories. Shuet helps him manage Jormund since Svaren is in the Thran's territory."

It was interesting. On the outside, they appeared to be mercenaries, but peel the layers and there was more to see. Perhaps the Rangers were worth investing in. Talyn studied Leif for a moment, then dismissed the thought.

No, it will be time to leave soon.

"Talyn?" Leif asked. "Something bothering you?"

Talyn blinked and looked around. They had pushed way past the gate and were deep in the village's interior. "Just lost in thought, Leif." The ranger shrugged and began tying Slep's reins to a post in front of a large building.

The village was quaint, but the buildings weren't much. Most were small but built in two levels, like all Sokoran structures. The first floor was dug into the ground with stairs leading down into it. It was used for storage during the winter and for living in the summer. It all depended on how bad the snows were year after year. Most used it for storage year-round.

"I'm going to talk to the village elder and see if they require anything," he said. "We can find a place to stay afterward. If they have nothing, we can leave for Yggsid in the morning."

***

Night or day was irrelevant, only the colors changed. At night, the 'light' was there, creating a twilight illumination. Thankfully, Leif had fallen asleep after meeting with Alif's elder. He seemed better now that he had let go of Brenja's death.

Talyn scanned the ruins and shook his head. In a way, they were a tragedy. What little remained of at one time had been a large city was barely noticeable. Most of the stone had eroded with the ravages of time, sunken into the earth or, as Leif had once explained, been carted off by Sokoran's for building materials. Mortals never seemed to have enough, except for Leif. He lived his life without such desires, or so it appeared.

"You dark elves and your ceaseless slaughter," he sighed. He closed his eyes, reaching out with his senses. They were there, deep in the snows below the earth. Entombed and trapped. "I bet you're out-raged, Keeper, at such a curse."

Memories surfaced. Talyn fought to discard them, refusing to allow them a moment to dredge of emotions best left buried. Coming to these lands was a mistake, but it seemed as if there had been no choice.

Whether by whim or fate, he was being pulled by a tether. Coming to Sokoras and ultimately visit Yggsid had been a flight of fancy, but the power he sensed, even at a distance from the ancient grove, was forcing his hand.

He looked up at the sky. As usual, the cloud cover had returned, obscuring the stars. "I miss the fact I don't get to see you often in this stupid country." He took one last look at the ruins, buried under mounds of snow and forest. "After tomorrow, I'll be seeing the stars once again."

***

Yggsid was strangely reminiscent of Daeshal. But unlike The Shadow Wood, the trees had been shaped and woven together to create the dense canopy. It wasn't a natural occurrence. The branches of the evergreens making up the grove gave an appearance similar to a large natural mound covering several acres. But whether by optical illusion or some other reason, it blended well with the rest of the forest.

Leif seemed to be in better spirits. After Alif, it didn't feel like there was much to say. The silence wasn't awkward, which was nice. The village elder had a request and was overjoyed that a ranger had been passing through.

Alif needed medicine and poultices that only Yggsid could provide. Lief happily agreed and thankfully, it gave them a better reason for being here. He had said that working their fields to barter for them would serve as payment.

Slep snorted as Lief pulled him to a stop at the grove's entrance. Two Shaylin stepped through the woven entrance moments later and bowed, crossing their arms across their chests. One was male and the other female, both dressed in heavy furs.

"Greetings, Ranger," the female said. "You don't appear to be one of Huntsman Wulf's."

"I was touring the smaller villages to see if they had any specific needs. I stopped in Alif yesterday. The elder asked me to acquire medicines and poultices from you."

The female nodded. "Are you planning to work the fields as payment?" she asked. "Elder Kala has little use for shards."

"I was and expected, no less," Lief replied politely.

"Then, if you dismount and follow me. Somasa will tend you your horse," she replied, gesturing to the Shaylin beside her.

Talyn froze for a moment, a strange sensation overtaking him. He glanced over at the two elves, feeling as if he were being watched, but neither appeared to notice him. 'Somasa', as the female had addressed him, was focused on Lief or seemed to be. The female was the same.

Inwardly, he cringed and tilted his head as a precaution, behaving more like a raven ought. Somasa's eyes shifted as he approached to take Slep's reins. The druid appeared concerned.

Is he aware of me?

The feeling grew after passing across the grove's entrance. Talyn gripped the tufts of Slep's mane between his talons. Something about this place was different. He could feel in his spirit. The groves in Daeshal weren't like this.

We may need to leave more quickly. I may not have the time Leif needs to complete his contract.

The female led Leif away, and while he tried to appear casual about it, Talyn could tell he was curious as to why they weren't staying together. He shifted his attention, observing Ygsidd's interior as the elf led Slep through the grove.

The grove's canopy reinforced the sense you were in a cave in the same way the great trees of Daeshal did. The evergreens were smaller, however, and their scent on the air was more pleasant. Some of the druid's homes had been built around or shaped within them. The design was rather beautiful and poetic.

Paths were molded with a natural aesthetic in mind, using stones of various sizes. For lighting, sun orbs were used. Placed along the paths, the druids had woven them into the trees, but set so they could be replaced easily enough. Like in the elves' homeland of Daeshal, they enchanted the orbs in time with the rotation of the sun. Despite his nausea, Talyn smiled inwardly. There was a sense of peace here.

After a while, Somasa came to a penned-in area where the druids kept some of their livestock. He led Slep to a row of stalls, stopping at the largest on the end where he began removing the horse's saddle and barding. With his height, it took some time and was comical to watch.

The druid was only about five and a half feet tall. Slep was twenty hands from ground to shoulder. Still, Somasa handled the task stoically. Once he was finished, Somasa organized all the tack and barding in a chest by the stall. Through the entire dance, the elf's behavior was odd. He seemed tense though, giving no indication that he'd seen a raven perched on Slep's head.

Talyn resisted the urge to sigh, though it was difficult. But grew concerned when the druid placed his hand on the doorway of the stall after closing the gate and began chanting softy. He traced his finger in a peculiar pattern and Talyn felt a wave of nausea wash over him. Somasa had just placed a ward.

Inwardly, Talyn's anger rose. *Impudent flea!*

Somasa looked about the stall, then walked away.

Talyn closed his eyes, letting his senses feel out the barrier. The magic was weak and easily sundered like parchment. He reached out, testing its bonds, then paused.

This is a trap. It's not a matter of if I can break, but rather a matter of when I break it. Talyn extended his senses further, pressing his awareness against the stall. The ward only covered the entrance, not the breaks between the planks making up the stall itself.

Talyn sighed and glided toward the wall. "*I hate snakes,*" he mumbled softly. Tapping into his power, Talyn's nausea grew. He felt his feathers peeling away, the cold air brushing against his skin as they shifted to scales. If snakes could vomit, he would have, as his tongue tasted the air during the transformation.

He could feel lethargy setting in as he slithered across the cold ground and sparse snow and through the break in the wall. Once through, Talyn shifted forms, becoming a raven. "Kin Selo," he whispered. *Try to sense me now, elf.*

Talyn stretched his awareness, searching the grove as far as they could extend. He felt a ping and took flight, homing in on its source. Whatever the creature was, it was close.

It didn't take long to find it. The source of the power was a human and a child at that. She was small and very young, between four or five years old at least, if he were to guess.

There were other children present. Some were human, while others Shaylin. They busied themselves with playing in a small clearing, chasing after one another. A few to gathered clumps of snow that had slipped through the canopy and tossed them at their peers. The little girl, however, was content to sit off to the side and watch. Sometimes she would laugh at them.

"Naya!" He heard someone shout. Talyn turned his head in the voice's direction. The woman it belonged to was human. Her hair was blonde, making her Sokoran. She was older, though.

The little girl's name was apparently Naya, because, at the sound of the woman's voice, she jumped up and ran toward the older human. The two embraced. It was almost endearing. The woman then held her hand out and Naya took it. The pair then turned toward one of the houses.

Talyn flew closer, moving from perch to perch as he followed them. The power radiating from the little girl made her potential clear. That alone made her dangerous and a threat. *He* would covet her if *He* ever awoke. Only those with her spark had that ability to wake Him.

"You poor human," Talyn whispered. *"You were cursed from the day you were born. I, however, will be merciful and keep you from His grasp. In my kindness, I will rob you of this innate spark gifted to you. Only then will you be beyond my former master's reach."*

Chapter Four

"You've come a long way, Ranger," she said.

Leif nodded. "It's been a tough winter on everyone this year. I've seen my fair share of terrible things."

The Shaylin paused, then turned to face him. "I think you have," she said, her eyes meeting with his. "Probably more than most."

Leif shuddered. Her tone carried a level of certainty, an edge that accented the look in her dark brown eyes. It was as if she were looking through him and found something lurking. Something she didn't like.

Shaylin were always hard to read, only the degree of emotion they showed hinted at their age. Still, by the same token, those same hints could be equally misleading. Elves prided themselves on their mastery at playing Kings, even if humans invented the game.

She turned away, her attention focused on the path. It was one of many. The others led deeper into the grove, each winding their own way toward some unknown destination. They were graded but like most in things in the grove; the pathways were natural, as if no tool had touched them.

Vibrant flowers with hues of blue, red, and purple lined their edges, granting them definition. It was like walking down a street, only greener. Thanks to the canopy overhead, it accented the sense that, even though it wasn't completely impenetrable from the snows, it separated the world outside and this one.

"We have a Shaper here," she chimed in. "Long ago it was a talent seen among many Shaylin. Now, it has become a rare thing. I fear it may fade one day, one more treasure lost to my people."

"I thought all druids could shape nature?" Lief replied.

"Not like a Shaper," she answered. Her tone resonated with reverence. "Druids coerce nature, bending it to their will. In rudimentary terms, we are simple carpenters. Shape and form are stimulated by our magic based on what we imagine. It takes talent, something few possess. The changes we make are never permanent. A Shaper, however, speaks to nature, asks it for aid, and becomes part of it."

"So you mean it becomes an expression of their desires?" Leif asked. "Of their hearts?"

She turned, briefly losing her footing, and catching herself. "You actually understand?"

"You sound genuinely surprised."

"Oh, I am," she said. "The humans we train to follow The Way understand, but for an outsider to grasp it..." She paused, narrowed her eyes. "I misjudged your ability to perceive things."

"These past few months have opened my eyes to many things. Perspective has been one of them."

She cracked a smile. "How curious." She took the lead once again, and they followed the path until it opened up to a small clearing. The canopy was denser here, only grass grew and the sun orbs around its perimeter provided warmth.

A handful of houses sat arrayed in a semi-circle. They weren't large, appearing capable of accommodating two people at most. Each was spaced within five yards of the other, but two houses were melded into part of the evergreens along the outer edge of the clearing.

"Huntsman Wulf reserved these for Rangers who might pass through, though he is currently away. I noticed you do not wear his banner."

"No, I receive my contracts from Huntsman Shuet," Leif replied.

"I will inform the Elders of your contract," she said. "You will need to make a list of the medicines you require. In exchange, a day working in the fields will suffice."

"When will I start?"

"In the morning and once you have bathed," she smirked. "You have the smell of a man who has been on the road far too long."

Leif grinned. "Here I thought such musk was a pleasing aroma to a woman."

"Only if you're a sow or desperate," she replied. "You may address me as Lennella."

"Then, you may address me as Leif."

She bowed her head respectfully, then started up the path. Leif turned toward the house, his attention drawn to the small raven perched on the roof.

"You know, I've always been fond of the grace Shaylin females carry about themselves. Especially how they smile. It's like getting stabbed in the back. Painful and bittersweet, surprising you and hurting all at once. Deep down you suspect the knife is there, but for some reason, you can't but help walk closer." Talyn shuddered. "Gets me every time."

Leif rolled his eyes. "Where did you run off to?"

"Nowhere in particular," Talyn replied. "This place unsettled me for a moment, but it's fine now."

Leif stopped halfway through the doorway of the small house. "Unsettled?"

Talyn flew through the doorway, passing him, and perched on the end of the bed. "This grove is just different," he said. "Its magic is strange."

Leif narrowed his eyes.

"What is it, Leif?" Talyn asked. "You look like something came to mind."

"Lennella told me there was a Shaper here."

A chill filled the room. Leif touched his chest and looked up at Talyn. He was angry. No, the small raven was terrified. The ranger's mouth felt open. *The Shaper can kill you.*

"Leif, finish your business quickly." His tone was the same as it had been in Gruiner before he had slain those three Blades. The weight of its authority was certain, radiating something primal, and insisting he should be obeyed.

Leif rubbed his temples. "Nothing has changed Talyn. You heard Lennella. A day's work and we leave."

"We will see," he replied coldly.

***

Yggsid was like the groves in Daeshal at night. The sun orbs were like lamps, providing just enough light for the Shaylin to see. The dimness of their light showed how late in the evening it was.

Pity for the humans, though. Some trained in The Way might have a nocturnal animal as their totem, making it easier to navigate in the dark like the Shaylin. Hopefully, none were about at this late hour.

Talyn stalked through the grove, keeping clear of the paths. He twitched his ears, every muscle tensed while listening for any aberrant sounds. There was none to speak of, just the eerie quiet blanketing the grove.

He curled his lip, the Shaper an ever constant in his mind. *How could I have not expected this? Of course, there would be a Shaper here.* House Ravenfeather always preferred for one at a grove if they can spare them. Though having one so far from the elves' homeland was unusual.

Why are you here?

He shook his head, shoving the questions aside. The task at hand came first. The Shaper was ultimately irrelevant. Only the child mattered. Her spark had to be extinguished.

Talyn stalked passed some of the communal clearings where many of the druids and their families lived until finally coming to the one Naya lived in. He looked up, feeling slightly foolish, when his gaze met with the canopy. Some habits were hard to break.

Talyn crept closer to the front door of her home, ears twitching as he listened for sounds of anyone stirring inside. Silence greeted him. Smiling, he crept around the house, toward the Naya's window.

"*Zgin'jesh,*" he whispered.

His feline frame became mist, and he drifted toward the window, seeping through the cracks. Once through, the incant ended, and he reformed, scanning the room to get his bearings. It was like he remembered, with a bit more clutter. It should be no surprise. She was very young.

A chest for her clothes sat at the foot of the bed. Her closet, where her mother hung her furs and winter clothing, was on the opposite side of the window behind him. Its large wooden frame and doors shaped by druidic magic. The seamless curves in its design were a telltale sign. Against the wall sat a spindle and other various tools for weaving and sewing.

Naya's mother was teaching her. She had the most curious expression when she practiced, but seemed to enjoy it. The little girl's toys littered the floor. Most were dolls made of wool and cloth. A set of them sat gathered around a large table and dressed like druid elders. It seemed 'the council' was in 'discussion'.

Talyn smirked, then shifted forms, transforming back into a raven, and taking flight. It was a quick hop onto the edge of the bed, though he was careful not to wake her. Staring at Naya, Talyn winced inwardly. *"Poor creature. I fear, like the Shapers so long ago, I must do the same to you."*

He closed his eyes, drawing on his power. Naya's spark resonated in response. It proved she was a Channeler and probably the first one to be born in nearly a millennium. Such power was humanity's last tie to their ancestors. To the Old Ones.

The air in the room grew heavy, his feathers shifting, like smoky shadows wafting in a breeze. Nausea returned in full force, but Talyn pushed past it, allowing the dark magic to swell inside his tiny body. Shadowy hands took shape above him. Hovering near his head. They seeming to absorb the ambient light filtering into the room from outside.

The dark hands stretched out, reaching toward Naya and plunging deep into her chest. Naya arched back in her bed, mouth open in a gasp for breath and eyes fluttering. Talyn simply looked on dispassionately. There would be no scream. No pain, at least nothing the body could understand or properly express.

"Though from ancient blood did you descend, a scar I leave that none can mend," he softly whispered. *"In shadow's hand, this spark is unkindled, and with its scarring touch you're your power has dwindled. Magic will be faint and out of reach, and to you, only the simplest magiks can your masters teach."*

The hands withdrew, one of them clutching a small red gem shard. Naya collapsed on her back, head turned to one side. She was still breathing, but unconscious.

Talyn opened his beak, turning his head up. The shadowy hand holding the red gem shard came closer and dropped it into his mouth. He craned his neck, swallowing it, then hopped off the bed and transformed into a snow leopard.

He winced. His body was already absorbing Naya's power into itself. *No! It's happening too quickly!*

"*Zgin'jesh,*" he whispered.

Transforming into a mist, he quickly slipped through the window. When he solidified outside, Talyn collapsed, clenching his jaw. The pain was intensifying. The sensation was like shards of glass slicing back and forth across his insides. He stretched out his front paws, clawing at the ground and fighting to get to his feet.

I need to get away!

Pushing through, as his fur fell away, Talyn sprinted toward the nearest evergreen. He leaped for the tree, burying his claws in it, and scaling up to its highest parts. His flesh already peeling and when he craned his neck, Talyn saw some of his claws had fallen out.

His vision blurred, and sense of smell vanished. Talyn went to take a step, but through the haze, saw that a cacoon had formed. He knew it anchored him to the evergreen now and would soon envelop him completely.

Talyn stopped fighting the change and gave in to the pain. He relaxed his will, like flexing a muscle, and his feline form melded into the cocoon's viscous membrane. After a few minutes, the pain numbed, and the cacoon washed over him. His sight had left him, his thoughts the only thing remaining.

Leif, pray they don't find me before your day is up.

***

Leif scanned the cleared and the canopy. Talyn had vanished. He pursed his lip, unable to shake the feeling that something was wrong.

"Not sleep well?"

He turned, trying to hide his surprise as Lenella seemed to appear from nowhere from the treeline. "No, I slept fine. I guess I'm not used to this place. It's so peaceful and serene."

Lennella smiled. "Many who visit Yggsid say that," she said. "Few realize how alive this grove is."

"Perhaps it's not the place but the people that bring it to life," Leif replied.

Her cheeks flushed, and she turned away, starting down the pathway. "Perhaps, Ranger," she said, sounding amused. "Now, shall we put you to work?"

Leif grinned. "Only if you insist." Maybe it was the grove, but part of him felt lighter. He glanced back at the house. *Talyn, please don't do something stupid here.*

***

He was unusual. Both as a human and a Ranger. Humans weren't the most thoughtful or introspective of creatures. They could be crafty and cunning when driven, but often those traits surfaced when they focused primarily on self and personal gain. It was bewildering. They had so much potential and talent, yet they waste it.

Rangers came to and went from the grove often enough. Some of them seeking Huntsman Wulf, while others were simply for a respite on their journeys. Generally, they were well-meaning, believed in what they did, and adhered to what the Rangers stood for. They often spoke about family, of the community they had created, and the brotherhood it represented. Still, Lenella couldn't help but feel that their true colors might show under the right circumstances. Loyalties among humans shifted as often as a winter breeze.

Looking at Leif, however, he seemed different somehow. There was something dark about him, but veiled behind many layers, and tempered with purpose. Whatever he had embraced because of it, that had become the source of his determination. Perhaps it had something to do with the Rangers themselves?

Though their interactions had been brief, Lenella was certain her latter assessment was correct and bled into him as a Ranger. The genuineness in his voice whenever he spoke. His sincerity in fulfilling his contracts. Leif believed in what he was doing. It wasn't like the others who had come passing through. Leif's convictions ran deeper.

Lenella smirked. He and Huntsman Wulf were similar. Like Leif, he was devoted to the cause, even if it sometimes caused tensions among the Elders. Wulf was a good man and leader. For a human.

She thought of Leif's blue eyes and how reminiscent of a raven's they were. While different in color, he was observant and watchful. Lenella bit her lip, unconsciously navigating the path.

What is this I sense from you? This hole inside?

"You seem deep in thought?" Leif commented.

Lenella blinked. "Am I?"

"It was hard to notice from the furs and folds of your robes at first, but you're tense," he said. "Though your back is turned, I briefly saw you biting your lip when we rounded that last bend."

She stopped, turning to face him. "Leif, why do I sense something dark lurking inside of you?"

He paused, his smile fading. "What do you mean?"

"You have a scar. It runs deep," she said. "What happened?"

And just like that, the mask he wore cracked. His blue eyes, telling their own tale. "We had best get to the fields," he replied solemnly.

Lenella drew closer, placing a gentle hand on his cheek. "Leif, whatever this thing is," she said. "You must let it go. It will only cause you more pain."

His expression grew hard. "We have work to do, Lenella."

"Of course, Leif," she replied. "Of course."

There wasn't much left to say after that. At last glance, Leif's expression said they were done talking. Despite the quiet walk to the caverns, upon their arrival, his expression changed upon seeing the immensity of the fields within them.

Everyone knew Yggsid was an essential part of helping the other territories survive. The food they grew year round benefited all. By the look he wore, it was obviously larger than what he had imagined.

Lenella grinned. "You were expecting something smaller."

"And colder," Leif replied, unclasping his cloak and gazing over the sea of green before him.

"While the greeneries in other villages use stoves and other means to heat and maintain the temperature," she said. "We use sun orbs. Their light nourishes and warms the plants."

"I've never seen so many," he replied, his tone hushed. "How long do they last? I've heard most only shine for three years at most."

"The ones in this cavern had been burning for twenty years now, I think."

His mouth felt open and Lenella smiled. He was like a boy with a renewed sense of wonder. Whatever cloud had hung over him was gone. It was endearing.

Lenella reached out, taking his left hand. Nervously, he complied, and she led him through the stalks of corn. "They're almost ready. In a few days, we'll begin harvesting them."

"How do you keep them from rotting?" he asked.

"Preservation Bags," she replied. "We make them. The magic doesn't keep them fresh indefinitely, but long enough to distribute them to the stores of the villages that need them."

"It feels like I really am in another world," he said.

Lenella gently squeezed his hand. "You could be," she replied. "For as long as you like."

His eyes softened. "Lenella…"

"I'm sorry for making you angry, Leif," she said. "My brother and I are more sensitive to things than most druids."

His eyebrows drew together as curiosity wound its way onto his face. "Sensitive how?"

"Sometimes, we Shaylin who train in The Way can feel more than just the energy and life of nature. Sometimes, we can feel what others do."

He looked away, his eyes fixed on the cornstalks behind her. "I really have stepped into a different world."

"Leif?"

He shifted his gaze. "Maybe I'll tell you as we work."

Lenella nodded. "Only if you are comfortable with it."

***

It was different, not having to keep bundled up. The heat the sun orbs provided was more than adequate. Leif paused, taking a breath and wiping the sweat from his brow. He caught a half-smile from Lenella when she glanced over her shoulder to watch him.

Like himself, she was covered in dirt and sweat, wearing a simple cotton tunic, pants, and leather slippers. Her soft auburn hair was pulled up in a bun and without it draped around her shoulders, Lenella's angular features and pointed ears were more pronounced. Leif caught himself struggling to keep from staring, though from the subtle tells she gave off, Lenella didn't seem to mind.

They had been working to prepare the ground for a new planting in what Lenella had dubbed 'The Southern Field'. Once the field was properly tilled and prepared, in another week, they would plant turnips. It was strange to think you needed to change what crops were planted throughout the year.

Thirty other druids worked alongside them. Most were quiet, with the occasional conversation between them. There were fewer Shaylin than expected as well. Lenella had said a few of her people lived in Yggsid. Most of the others were Sokoran and had resided in Yggsid for generations.

"I've noticed the sun orbs dimming."

Lenella glanced over at one of the closest orbs mounted on an iron pole. "I never realized it was so late," she commented.

Leif smiled. She sounded a bit disappointed. "You sure you aren't trying to work me to death?"

A wicked smirk crossed her face. "Well, we could always use more fertilizer for the fields. Perhaps I will simply have to leave you guessing about my intent."

Leif shook his head, a broad grin on his face. "I suppose I will simply have to keep a sharper eye, preferably before I pass out."

She smiled wider. "If you do, then you are fortunate to be surrounded by so many who can nurse you back to health."

Leif sat back, laughing. The feeling from earlier returned, the one of a dark shroud lifting from his shoulders. Lenella had already turned her attention back to her work, but her smile never faded. She was biting her lip again.

A loud gong sounded, and one by one, the druids began gathering their tools. Leif began collected up the spades, trowels, and rakes. Lenella took to gathering the loose canvas sacks used to haul fertilizer for the fields. They loaded everything into a small wagon sitting on a nearby dirt path. It was one of several used like small roads to travel between fields in the cavern.

Leif carefully stacked the tools in a pile in the wagon, then turned to Lenella, taking the sacks of fertilizer from her. The putrid stench of their former contents assaulted his nostrils as he fought the urge to gag. Lenella laughed, and he tossed one of the sacks onto her head.

"Ugh!" she cried out, grabbing the sack and throwing it back at him. "You horrid man!"

Leif chuckled, catching it. "It'll wash out."

She rolled her eyes, trying to hide her smile. Some of the other druids cracked a few smiles of their own, while others simply shook their heads. Leif tossed the sack into the back of the wagon and began pushing it toward the entrance to the cavern. He felt a hand touch his shoulder and looked back to see Lenella shaking her head.

"You can leave it there. Someone will be along after the evening meal to finish up," she said.

"Are you sure? It's not that far."

She nodded. "Everyone in the grove does their part. We have a lot more to do tomorrow."

The disappointment in her voice returned. Leif felt a twinge in his chest. There would be no work tomorrow. Talyn would want to leave before first light.

He smiled softly, shoving his feelings aside. "Lead the way, fair lady."

***

The mood had shifted since leaving the fields. It was like before it had been that morning, before reaching the caverns. Leif appeared to be deep in thought and some of his emotions were bleeding through.

The most powerful among them was regret. He wanted to stay, but something was preventing him from following his heart. Lenella touched her chest, a sense of foolishness washing over her.

You can't expect him to stay. You can't heal that hole inside him.

"It was seven years ago," he said.

She paused and turned on the path to face him.

"I was tracking a Blade up north. He had gotten into a fight and killed someone in a drunken fit," he said. "It was my first bounty. I had just earned the right to accept contracts on my own." He bit his lip, his expression hardening and eyes watering. "I was such a stupid kid."

Lenella drew closer, cupping his face in her hands. "Tell me, Leif, let it go," she said, tilting his head down and resting her forehead against his.

"He deserted and normally Bodvar would hunt his own, but the man killed one of our own. Shuet felt it was best handled by another Huntsman because of Viktor. Eirik was livid, but allowed it."

"So you found him?"

He nodded. "I found him. He was trying to book passage to Absion. Things went bad from there."

Lenella felt her eyes water. More emotions were bleeding through. Leif's dam burst, leaving his regret and guilt flowing freely.

"I chased him throughout Yodnar, but everyone knows it's futile to run from us. By the end of my hunt, he had taken a hostage."

"She died, didn't she?"

He looked away. "I knew she might die, but I was so focused on the bounty, on the attack on our *family*, that I got careless. When it was done, I killed him too. No one would question it. He was a Blade."

"Leif, look at me," she said. When their eyes met, Lenella leaned in and kissed him. "I forgive you. You've suffered from this long enough, Leif."

Leif collapsed on the path, his embrace like a vise. He was crying. "I have lived with the memory that day for a long time. I swore I would never make the same mistake again."

She held him tight. Leif simply let the tears come. The flood of emotions pouring from his heart was long overdue. What he had done was wrong, but it explained his devotion to the Rangers. They were his penance.

"*I'm here, Leif,*" Lenella whispered, softly stroking her fingers through his dark hair. "*I'm here for as long as you need.*"

***

Though the light was dim, it may as well have been broad daylight. Its brilliance seared his eyes with each new tear that formed across the cacoon. Talyn wanted to scream but fought the urge. Instead, he summoned his powers to cloak himself in darkness.

He pressed against the chrysalis, its confines resisting. Slowly it sheared and with it sundered, the cold air of the outside world filled his lungs.

Taking it in, Talyn focused, pooling his energy into maintaining his feline form.

He dismissed the darkness, his eyes adjusting to the light. He looked down and frowned. *Poor, poor, Shaylin,* he thought after his eyes met with Somasa's, who was looking up at him from the ground. *You should have left things alone.*

Chapter Five

Leif trembled, soaking in the warmth of Lenella's naked body pressing against him. He closed his eyes, absorbing the sensation and yearning for every ounce she could offer. He smiled as Lenella slept, her hot breath against his bare chest sending ripples through him. It was tempting to wake her and start the dance anew. No doubt existed that she would be willing.

He opened his eyes, drinking in her sharp angular features, almond-shaped eyes, and dark brown hair. It was hard not to imagine anything more beautiful while staring at her. *"I don't want to leave you,"* he softly whispered.

She stirred, holding him tighter, but didn't wake. Leif glanced at the table. Two plates, a large pot, and a pitcher of ale sat atop it. There was still food in the pot. Lenella had prepared it. Dinner, however, had been brief.

After the moment they shared on the path, everything between them changed. Her feelings were plain. Shaylin were like that. They didn't layer things, well that is to say they act on their feelings. Her mind had been made up since working the fields together.

Gently, Leif stroked her hair. A warm smile crept its way onto her olive cheeks. His heart pounded, desire rising like a fountain. The past few months with Talyn felt like a dream. A thing that could be forgotten.

I was never the one watching you, was I, Talyn? Leif stared at the ceiling. The thought wasn't new, but admitting the truth cut deep.

"Leif?"

He turned his head. Lenella was awake. Her soft brown eyes were full of tenderness and warmth. She took his hand, pressing it against her cheek, gently nuzzling it.

"I like how they feel," she said, closing her eyes. "It is the touch of a man who works hard."

Leif let his right hands drift down to the small of her back under the blankets. She gasped softly, soaking it in, then smiled wickedly.

Her smile curved slightly more. "Someone's awake..." she commented "... and eager."

Leif pulled her up, leaned in, and kissed her forehead. "I can't help it. I don't remember the last time I felt this way."

She slid her arm around him, nuzzling against him. "What way is that?"

Leif gently stroked her hair. "Whole," he replied. "I never realized how much I let that day drive me. It consumed so utterly. I never wanted to be responsible for getting another killed. I let that woman die, Lenella."

"I know, Leif," she said. "And you've spent all this time torturing yourself for it."

"It doesn't feel enough. Now that I've admitted it. I keep thinking I should turn myself into Shuet."

She clutched him tightly. Leif did the same. Everything had happened so quickly between them. She, in true Shaylin fashion, had committed herself to her emotions and feelings. There weren't any doubts or worries. Only the moment, the present, existed.

"What would that prove?" she asked. "Your human laws in this country are strict. You would be disavowed and executed."

She stretched to the floor and closed her eyes. Her lips moved, but there were no words. The floorboards twisted, molding themselves as if they were clay. At first, buds grew, then in moments a small sapling about a foot in length grew from them. It was seamless; no, effortless more appropriately described what he witnessed.

"The Cycle turns, Leif," she said. "Many interpret it differently. Some see change within it. Some see the natural order of things. Regardless, it is in motion. You were born, serving the Rangers with zeal and fire. Then, the woman died and part of you died with her. You spent so much time clinging to this death that your place in The Cycle became incomplete. Now, you have been reborn."

Leif winced. "It's not that simple, Lenella."

She clenched her hand into a fist. The sapling blackened, withered, then died. "But it is. Everything is a cycle, Leif. Life, death, and rebirth. Change in life is constant. Punishing yourself for the past won't.

I left Daeshal because there were some of my grove who could not let something go. They tried and clung to an ancient tree, hoping to revive it. But I saw the truth and acted, ending the perpetual suffering they were causing."

"*You're the Shaper,*" he softly whispered.

She nodded. "I am. My brother and I both. The Elders were furious that I had slain the oldest tree in our grove. While I was simply returning it to the Cycle, they saw it as an abomination. To me, it was time. I could hear it suffering."

Her eyes watered and a single tear trickled down her cheek. Leif sat up, pressing into Lenella and kissing her. The blankets fell away, and she clung to him, kissing him passionately.

Leif pulled away, catching his breath. "*So, you have no home to return to?*" he whispered, staring into her eyes.

Lenella shook her head. "No, we can never return to The Wood. Yggsid is our home now," she replied. "I took a life, Shaper or not, to the grove and in the eyes of House Ravenfeather, I disrupted The Cycle."

"Why don't they react the same way here?"

"Sokoras is a different land and Yggsid a different place. House Ravenfeather helped found it a very long time ago, but no longer sees the grove as part of its responsibilities. The Shaylin who live here now were born from those who decided to stay and help the humans."

"To them, Yggsid is there home," he said.

"It is. Daeshal is just another place as far as they are concerned."

Lenella turned, positioning herself so her back was against his chest, and pulled the blankets up to cover them both. Leif wrapped her arms about her waist and rested his chin on her shoulder. In response, her soft hands and arms came to a rest atop his own.

Talyn, just stay away. Don't come back.

"How is this so simple?" he asked.

Lenella tilted her head, looking up at him from the corner of her right eye. "Because it is. I have chosen you, Leif. You are different and with that choice, I committed myself to you."

"What does that even mean?"

She wove her fingers into his. "It means that for me, there will not be another. While there are rare exceptions, we Shaylin, once we have chosen a mate, are paired for life. For us, there can never be another. Our spirits are bound as one. Unlike humans, we take intimacy more seriously."

"But how do you know me?" Leif asked. "How can you know I can commit to something like that?"

"Because I feel it," she replied. "Your heart is desperate to be vulnerable, to let go and be embraced by another honestly. Your sins, faults, and hurts all of it. You want to be free and know that such grace exists."

Leif held his breath. She was right. No one had ever put into words what had driven him for so long. "Lenella..."

"I know Leif," she said. "A shadow hangs over you still and it will do anything to keep you within its clutches."

He froze. Questions assaulting him. Leif bit his lip, nausea gripping him as the impulse to silence her welled up within him. Another sign of Talyn's influence.

He fought it, casting it aside. *No, I can't. No matter what happens, I can't.*

"Leif," she said. "I can help you, but you have to choose. No matter what happens, you are my mate now. That will never change."

He held her tight. "I want to choose you. More than anything."

***

He was an elusive one, this druid, but also a fool. He had failed to alert anyone and chosen to run straight for where Leif was staying. Talyn trembled, chills running through him from the smell of elven blood in the air. Somasa had fought well. As a Shaper his magic was potent.

In the back of his mind, he questioned why Somasa had run for Leif's lodgings. Was he so naïve to think that he would find sanctuary there? Talyn winced, his shoulder stabbing at him in pain. No, the druid was too smart for that.

The shapeshifter crept through shadows, enshrouded by the darkness his form offered. Using it was risky. The druids would sense the corruption such dark magic would leave in its wake. A few of the plants and trees along the path had already begun withering.

Shadow magic was like that. It could take life just by being close to it. The malice and hunger of its nature insatiable. Talyn fought back the nausea. It was a byproduct of becoming a creature steeped in such dark power.

"Somasa," he whispered. *"Come out and play. I'm hungry."*

The grove was quiet. Somasa's scent said he was close. The smell of blood was growing stronger. Judging by the distance, they were near the house Leif was staying in. The path would end soon.

The sound of something whipping through the air drew his attention. Talyn turned just as the forest came alive and vines surged toward him, binding his shadowy form. Their very touch was like acid against his body. Some became like spears, stabbing at him.

He clenched his beak, resisting the urge to screech in pain. *"Xiv Sha!"*

The vines wilted, becoming blackened paste, and he shook the residue off, craning his neck to scan the forest. He grunted, pain shooting up his *spine*. The puncture wounds from the vines weren't closing.

He dropped to all fours. The sparse grass and flowers at his underneath his talons immediately wilting at his touch. *Stupid elf, I'm going to absorb every drop of your essence!*

Talyn closed his eyes, focusing on the scent of Somasa's blood. He was moving away. At this rate, he would reach Leif first.

So it's attrition, little Shaper. You're trying to whittle away at me bit by bit. He reached for the nearest tree, clutching it in his large talon. The flow of life siphoning away from it was sweet. Talyn could already feel his wounds closing. The tree withered, groaning under its own weight before turning to ash.

Run elf, we will end you!

***

There had been no explanation. Lenella had simply jumped from the bed and donned her clothes. She stood on the porch of the small house, her eyes fixed on the path leading into the grove. Leif shivered, wishing he wore more than just a pair of cloth pants and a tunic. He gripped his shortblades, standing protectively in front of her.

Moments later, thanks to Talyn's gift, Somasa came into view from the darkness. He was panicked, with blood running down his face, his appearance emaciated like a fern addict, but with his senses seemingly intact. It took Lenella a little longer to notice him, but when she did, the Shaper ran toward her brother as he collapsed at the end of the path.

"*It comes!*" he groaned.

"Leif!" she shouted.

Leif ran toward her, planting his shortblades into the ground and taking the young druid into his arms. Together, they rushed toward the porch and laid him close to the doorway. Lenella knelt beside her brother, placing her hands over his wound. A glow emanated from her palms, his wounds slowly closing.

Leif turned to the treeline by the path and locked his jaw. Even though he could sense it, the ranger knew Talyn was coming, and he was angry. Through whatever bond they shared, the shapershifter's murderous intent was plain. He rushed toward the path, where his swords lay planted, and scooped them up.

"Leif!" Lenella shouted. "You must reject him! His hold cannot last!"

"*My hold?*" His voice was deep, power resonating in its tone. "*Didn't he tell you, little whore? He chose me, accepted me, long before you took him on your leisurely evening ride!*"

Leif planted his feet, the cold seeming to vanish as his heart pounded. The trees groaned, the sound of them toppling sounding in his ears. This wasn't like before in Grunier.

"*I hope you had your fun, Shaper,*" he said. "*I despise thieves, elf! Leif. Is. Mine!*"

Leif stepped back. The trees and ground near the path were turning black. They were dying and once they collapsed, in the dim light of the crescent moon, Talyn revealed himself. In form, he was a shadow-like creature, something between a raven and a wingless griffon. He was as large as an ice bear, his eyes glowing with a haunting pale light.

There was something off about the creature he had become. The form didn't seem stable, as if he were fighting to maintain its shape. Shadowy feathers would sprout from his front limbs and his size grew slightly larger before reverting to normal. It was like his body was trying to transform into some great bird of prey, but Talyn was fighting against it.

It must be exhausting to keep that up.

"Leif," Talyn said, his voice less ominous. "You had your pleasures. Now end this and let's move on. We have places to be."

Leif stepped forward, a wave of exhaustion rolling over him. "I'm not killing anyone Talyn!"

The familiar tilted his head and narrowed his eyes. "Kill them, or I will." His tone was the same as it was at the plantation, though devoid of the pity he showed then. "You can't possibly love her. You're a human. A fickle, small, human. You aren't like them."

Staring into his eyes and seeing him in that form, Leif felt the weight of Talyn's hold. He glanced back at Lenella. Her attention focused on saving her brother. Her face was a mask as she used her magic to heal him.

"Do it, Leif, kill them. Be who you are, be who I saw, and see now."

"No, I have made my choice," he replied. "I choose her."

Talyn craned his neck low, ripples rolling through his shadowy form. It was like watching water flow or fire dance about. "Then I will end this. You are *mine*, Leif. Mine for eternity."

He stepped forward, but Leif intercepted him.

"Stand too close and you will die, Leif," Talyn said. "I will leech the very life out of you!"

"Then you will once again be alone."

Strangely, Talyn stepped back. He seemed hesitant. "I have always been alone, Leif."

Leif looked back toward Lenella. She looked exhausted. Whatever Talyn had done to her brother wasn't something that one could simply heal. He leaned over, taking his shortblades and drawing a long line on the ground. He then planted them at either end.

"You will not cross this line, Talyn!"

The familiar said nothing. Instead, he stared at the line, eyes narrowed. Leif turned his back, pausing briefly. Talyn was irritated, but why?

He walked up to the house and knelt beside Lenella. "I'm sorry. I never wanted this."

She looked up, eyes soft and full of grace. "I know," she replied. "That creature does not belong in this world. It deceives and tricks to get its way. It may hide itself from others, but I can sense its nature."

"I cannot stay. I'm not strong enough to stop him," he replied.

"But you are Leif," she said. "You gave him the power over you. Together, we can take it back."

"I can't. He'll kill you. I can't bear that."

A tear fell down her cheek. "I know," she replied. "I had hoped you would stay, but in my heart, I knew you would leave."

"Then why choose me?" Leif asked. "Why decide that someone un reachable was to be your mate?"

"Because I see you too," she replied. "I chose you to give you an anchor on your journey. Something that he cannot take away."

Leif swallowed hard and pressed his lips against hers. "I will return to you."

She shook her head. "No, you won't, but I will wait regardless. For me, there can never be another."

"One day, Lenella, I will return and we will have whatever is left of my life together."

She smiled warmly, tears flowing. "Then I will wait for you. Even into my Twilight."

***

Leif gripped Slep's reins while staring at the Coldfire Mountains as they drew closer. Smoke rose from deeper within the range. The active volcanoes and unstable terrain made traveling them dangerous.

"You'll love Absion, Leif," Talyn beamed. "Well, minus the horrid heat and judgemental stares of their pompous Inquisitors. The gladiatorial fights are entertaining enough, however. Oh, and there's the Shaed-zlen..."

"Talyn, be silent." The familiar immediately clammed up, anger radiating in his eyes.

Leif smiled. The answer had been so simple. Talyn had once been someone's familiar. Such creatures were bound to do whatever was commanded of them when ordered directly. It was a secret the raven had hidden from him.

The commands had to be specific, however. Talyn was clever and would twist things to his advantage. The bond wasn't absolute.

I promise to come home to you, Lenella. There will be no one else for me.

***

"How are you feeling, Sister?"

Lenella shifted in the recliner, softly touching her belly. "Better today. The little one isn't kicking quite so hard."

Somasa leaned on his cane, only half-smiling. He wasn't happy with the pregnancy, but life was life. Whatever the child was to be born as, human or elf, it was family.

She studied her brother, feeling a twinge at the sight of his wooden leg beneath the folds of his robes. They had shaped it together. The prosthetic would move like a real leg, though he still needed the cane for balance. His original leg had been beyond aid that night.

Somasa's breathing was still strained, even after eight months. The fight with Talyn had scarred his lungs. The dark magic the creature wielded kept them from fully healing.

"Have you settled on a name?" he asked.

Lenella blinked, his question bringing her back to the present. "Lal Thala for a girl."

Somasa cocked an eyebrow. "Interesting. And what of a boy?"

"Ta Lal."

His expression was thoughtful, but offered little else. "Moon's Light and Heart's Light," he said. "Let us pray to The Lady that the child lives up to its name."

THE WOLF AND THE MOON

An icy wind whipped through the dire wolf pens as Asger tended to the pack. The pen was part of a quintet and one of many found throughout Sergerard's walls. The dire wolves eagerly tore into the chunks of yak meat left in the trough, some snapping at each other while vying for dominance, but nothing too serious to force the young warrior to intervene.

He paused as the Sokoran air bit his ears and nose. Pride touched his heart while eying the buildings and homes around him. Sergerard was larger than most villages within Thran Henrik's territory, with a population of close to two hundred. Though for reasons he couldn't fathom, his lord had forbidden it from being marked on any map.

As the thick clouds overhead parted and the light of the full moon spread across the village, the dire wolves in the pens stopped eating or milling about and howled. More across the village joined in the chorus, the night air filling with their cries.

The young warrior listened, part of him wondering why they always did so on nights when the moon was the fullest and the clouds were thin enough to see the pale sphere in the sky. As if to remind him he shouldn't stand around pondering such things in the open, another icy wind blew through.

A storm was coming, but here in the north, that was no surprise. Storms from the Peridith Sea were common, as was the thick layer of snow always blanketing the ground. Asger eyed the chimney stacks of the other homes scattered about the village, longing for the warmth of his own hearth. The wolves, however, needed tending to.

The sound of the door to the quintet drew him. "They are calling to her."

Asger turned to Brandt, the old, grizzled leader of Segerard's wolf riders, as he entered the pen by the gate. "Calling to who?" he asked.

"Aluna, well, that's what the southerners call her," Brandt replied. "We know her as Aruna."

"But we rarely see Aruna. She always hides behind her brother, Eske."

"Aye, that be true, boy, but they know," Brandt said, pointing to the dire wolves in the pen. "They see her on the nights of the full moon, when Eske is at his brightest."

"But how?"

The old wolf rider grinned. "Because they remember their ancestor's love for her." Asger gave him a quizzical look, and Brandt laughed. "Don't tell me your Da never told you the story of the Wolf and the Moon?"

Asger frowned. "Da, never says much. He's always drinking."

Brandt tightened his lip, casting an awkward glance at the dire wolves in the pen before turning back to Asger. "I'm sorry, boy, that was harsh of me."

"The truth is a harsh thing," Asger replied, walking close to the closest dire wolf and petting it. The beast lowered its head, allowing him to scratch it between the ears. "But our homeland is full of harsh truths."

"I'll never get used to seeing that," Brandt commented, noting how the wolf allowed Asger to walk up to it so casually. "I don't understand why you don't go to Yggsid to drain with the druids."

Asger gave him a reluctant smile. Even when he was young, the wolves always treated him like one of their own. Many in the village took it as a sign of The Lady's favor. "Because my place is here, in Sergerard. I serve our people and I serve Henrik."

Brandt smiled. "Spoken like a true Rider."

Asger took a breath, the cold biting his lungs. "So, the story?" he asked, snuggling close to a wolf for warmth. The wolf, in turn, gave an approving groan, licking his face. Had he not shifted his weight, the beast would have knocked Asger over.

"Brandt, the story?"

The older warrior nodded. "This took place long before we were here, before even the fabled Aetharians and our enemies, the Norens. When the land wasn't this awful frozen land we know," he began. "

***

The sound crunching snow beneath Mangarmyr's paws helped dull the silence of the forest. He eyed the landscape, gaze drifting between the smattering of evergreens and pines. This was his territory. His domain.

But as trudged through his kingdom, his heart ached. Mangarmyr knew he was different from his own kind. He was smarter and more cunning than other Garou. They shunned him, females included. So he hunted in solitude, wandering his domain with neither pack nor companion for comfort.

He looked to the sky, to the stars shining brightly above. There were no clouds. Just a pristine blanket of starlight. "Are you hiding up there?" he whispered. "Adoshen, where have you gone?"

The stories say Father had vanished. Some still prayed to him, hoping he would answer like in the days of old, like in the First Dawn and sometimes in the Second. Yet, in El'Anthar's Third Dawn, Adoshen remained silent. The world had never been the same since.

"Mother used to say that you talked to all of us once, listened to our hearts and spoke so intimately with us, Father. The others have forgotten you. They call me foolish. But I still hope."

The Garou's gaze drifted across the night sky until two large pale orbs appeared. One lagged behind the other, as if hiding, yet daring to peek past it. He stared at them, his brown eyes filling with their light. They outshone the stars, softly illuminating the night.

The second orb shone a hair brighter. It's light reaching deep into his heart. "Who are you? What are you?"

No sooner were the words spoken than the twin orbs vanished and another wind blew, but the scent it carried made Mangarmyr's hackles rise. The aroma was tainted, corrupt, like a corpse left to rot. Demons...

Mangarmyr snarled, bearing his fangs. Ever since the Third Dawn, when the world broke, The Fallen have crept into El'Anthar from the shadows, spreading their malice and hate. The Old Ones had become a near memory, skulking to places where none could find them.

While they hide, El'Anthar crumbles and the Lurantiel suffer. *So many of us have fallen. So many of the Eldest gone. It shouldn't be this way!*

The Eldest were the most powerful among the spirits. They were with Adoshen before El'Anthar was formed. Many were now lay asleep, healing from the conflict at the end of the Second Dawn. A few went mad as the world fell out of balance, unable to cope with the distortion left in the wake of the Fallen.

Others changed, becoming more powerful and dangerous. The Fallen feared them the most. As their powers grew, so too did they change in form. While the Lurantiel could end a demon and banish it. The Eldest, like the old ones, could end its existence entirely.

The smell of demonic taint wafted on the air, much closer than before. Mangarmyr pivoted, his eyes falling on a black wolf with spines running the length of its back. *Fenrir!*

The fallen spirit snarled; red eyes gleaming. "A lone Garou," it mused. "Such easy prey."

Mangarmyr rose to his full height, chest puffed out. "I am far from easy prey, wretch." The sound of crunching snow touched his ears, and the Garou froze. Two more Fenrir lurked at the edge of his vision.

"The cub looks lost," one sneered. "So alone."

"We heard that there was one who controlled these woods, but such a small thing doesn't impress," the other chimed in.

"Them come, let me show you filthy things, why none tread here."

The three of them lunged, jaws wide. Mangarmyr dashed backward, using his front paws to flip and land on his feet. The Fenrir on either side of him crashed into each other, while the third bounded past them, using bodies as a springboard to pounce.

Closing the distance, while his enemy was in the air, Mangarmyr angled his jaws, clamping them around the Fenrir's throat. His teeth sank deep, crushing the fallen spirit's windpipe. Surprise shone in the Fenrir's eyes as it died, but Mangarmyr didn't have time to think.

The other two Fenrir were already up, fangs bared, their crimson eyes full of hate. "We'll shred you and feast on your essence!"

Mangarmyr curled his lip. *Spirits feeding on their own kind...* He charged them and they tensed, then separated to flank him. Mangarmyr shot past, waiting for the attack that would come from behind. But it didn't. The Fenrir had vanished.

He spun, senses on alert. Something was wrong. Fenrir couldn't vanish without enough shadow to conceal them. The area was too open and lacked the darkness they needed to stage an ambush. Drawing on his magic, Mangarmyr called up a gust of icy wind, sending snow flying and granting him cover. He listened to the wind, feeling out its pattern for subtle shifts.

Patience, he told himself. Instinct bucked. His sense of danger growing. *Patience,* he repeated. Other Garou would have handled things more violently, allowing instinct to overtake reason. They would have used their power sooner, with devastating effect.

Alone and separated from their pack, most would have run. Though such action meant death and losing oneself. They would return to The Cycle, as all spirits do, but who they were would be lost, only to be reborn later.

The wind shifted, breaking the pattern. Mangarmyr saw movement amid the snow flurries, the scent of taint wafting from the Fenrir crawling up his nostrils. He fell to his belly as a set of jaws snapped at him, then rolled, coming to his feet. The wind and snow came to a sudden halt.

His enemies stood before him, covered in frost. It matted itself firmly in their fur. Judging by their hateful stares, both fallen spirits were in pain. *How pitiful... The cold is nothing to the Garou.*

Mangarmyr crouched low, and the Fenrir mirrored him. Seconds later, they vanished. The great wolf blinked in confusion, but that moment was all his enemies needed. The Fenrir reappeared, but this time he was too slow.

Their fangs found their mark, sinking into his flank and side. Mangarmyr howled, immediately craning his neck afterward, and clamping his jaws around the throat of the one biting into his side. The Fenrir yelped just as his throat was torn out.

The other bit harder, teeth sinking deeper. Mangarmyr collapsed, fighting to pull himself up, but his right leg wouldn't respond. Seeing Mangarmyr hampered, the Fenrir let go, licking the blood from its snout.

"You are strong, cub. Feasting on you and my brothers will strengthen me. This forest will be mine, as will the world beyond."

"World beyond?" Mangarmyr panted.

The Fenrir laughed. "The dead don't need to know. Maybe in your next Cycle you'll find out."

The fallen spirit turned to where its kin lay and, dragging the corpses to one place, tore into each in turn. Mangarmyr growled as he watched the gristly scene. *Spirits eating their own kind...*

Mangarmyr waited, focusing his magic. The Fenrir believed he had won.

The fallen spirit's eyes took on an unholy light. Its fur thickening as it fed, swallowing chunks of flesh from its dead packmates, and leaving very little left. The sheer gluttony of the scene made Mangarmyr want to heave. It then turned, staring hungrily at the wounded Garou, pausing briefly, eyes drifting to the snow around Mangarmyr.

"Clever," it snapped. "You thought I wouldn't sense it, but I can wait. You will bleed to death soon enough before you heal from your wounds." It lay down, front paws crossed. "Now bleed for me, little Garou, and drift off to oblivion."

Your kind are so arrogant, especially when they think they've won!

By the time the Fenrir realized what was happening, it was too late as the snow underneath him came to life and impaled him. In the seconds before the shards appeared, the fallen spirit tried to react, moving mere inches, before the ground erupted underneath him. While that alone kept him from dying immediately, the Fenrir understood his fate was sealed.

"Clever," he rasped. "You distracted me by infusing your power into the snow around your body. You knew I would sense it."

Weakly, Mangarmyr got up, pain shooting through his right hip. "It's time to purify you."

The Fenrir sneered. "One day you'll fall too. The weight of this world will become too much for the Garou and only we, Fenrir, will remain."

Breathing deep, Mangarmyr exhaled a white mist, covering the Fenrir in it. The fallen spirit snarled, then yelped in pain, before becoming translucent and vanishing. Not even a trace of its blood remained.

Mangarmyr turned to the corpses of the Fenrir's packmates. There wasn't much to work with, but he hoped at least it would be enough to purify them back into The Cycle. Otherwise they would be reborn as Fenrir, corrupting everything around them. Exhaling the same mist, like the other Fenrir, they dissipated, leaving nothing behind.

Mangarmyr collapsed, eyes growing hazy. He tilted his head, left eyes focusing on the stars. The two pale orbs once again hung in the night sky. The second still lagged the first, yet more it of showed. "I don't know who you are, spirit, but I sense you. If you have no name, I will call you Aruna. It means 'beautiful light'."

The newly named orb gave no response. Perhaps it wasn't a spirit after all. Mangarmyr laid on his left side, pain stabbing him in the hip. It was growing harder to keep his eyes open, each breath shortening.

"I wish we could have met under better circumstances, Aruna," he panted. "You're the first thing to warm my heart in a very long time."

Inwardly the Garou laughed at himself. *You're talking to a strange thing in the heavens, Mangarmyr.* He closed his eyes, ready to embrace his time. He would reborn and perhaps finally find a pack and a mate. Though it also saddened him, what made him who was would be gone forever.

"Goodbye, Aruna," he said. "Whatever you are, I hope you live a better life than me."

***

Through the pain and haze, Mangarmyr briefly glimpsed a pale blur. The sound of wood banging together softly touched his ears, but he was too weak to fully open his eyes. Whatever the creature was, it moved strangely and not on all fours. He tried to speak, but his body wouldn't yield. Fatigue had a firm hold on him.

I've lost too much blood, he thought.

"Just rest," a soft voice said. It sounded female, lacking the depth and range of a male's.

He felt her touched his hip, and he tensed, but there was no pain. "Rest brave wolf. You've earned it."

A fog crept over the Garou's mind as sleep and fatigue tightened their grip. Mangarmyr fought them, but he knew he was too weak to resist and eventually, he passed out.

***

The warmth of the fire licking Mangarmyr's muzzle was like a breath of fresh air, or the distant memory of his mother nestling him close to her in the winter. Young cubs didn't share their parent's resilience for the cold. It was something they grew into.

When he opened his eyes, the Garou saw the strangest creature. It walked on two legs, but had no fur, save for on its head. The creature's fur hung loosely. Down to the middle of what he assumed was its back. It covered itself in something, reminding him of the stories he had heard of the old ones. They wore something called 'clothes', a kind of removable skin, at least as he once imagined it. But the scent they carried held faint traces of sheep's wool on them.

As he observed it, Mangarmyr found its lack of a muzzle bizarre. Even the creature's nose was attached directly to its face. "What are you?"

It paused, adjusting its coverings as if the cold bothered it. *Mother, these clothes you described aren't like I imagined. You said they made them from plants, but I smell sheep on this creature.*

"I am Aruna," it replied. The voice was the same female voice he remembered hearing before.

Her lips parted, showing her teeth. These were stranger than the rest of her. Most were blunted, lacking any sharp edge. There were hints of canines, but they were much too short to pierce anything. In fact, Mangarmyr wondered if Aruna ate meat at all.

Mangarmyr sat up, resting on his belly, surprised there was no pain. He craned his neck, glancing at his hip. There wasn't even a scar. "You helped me..."

Aruna nodded, showing her teeth again. By the gesture, the Garou assumed Aruna was trying to offer comfort, but it was a curious behavior. "Why do you bare your teeth at me?" he asked. "You would threaten someone you're helping?"

She laughed. "It's called a smile. It's used for different things, like expressing joy, comfort and pleasure, for example."

Mangarmyr thoughtfully shifted his attention to the fire, then turned to her and tried smiling. She became hysterical, laughing so hard she held her sides.

"What did I do?" He asked. "Was that not a smile? I am grateful for helping me."

Aruna closed the distance between them and wrapped her limbs around Mangarmyr. "You're so adorable. It was a good attempt, but I don't think your muzzle was meant for smiling."

While probably true, Mangarmyr couldn't help but feel a sliver of disappointment. He'd never heard of this smile before, but it was new and interesting. Maybe it might help him find a mate.

Aruna seated itself beside him. "What are you, Aruna? I have never seen a creature like you. Are you a new spirit? Has Adoshen returned?"

"I am human, but also something more now. This is how I looked once, a long time ago."

It wasn't a no, may Adoshen had returned, but something else also struck Mangarmyr. Aruna is sad... he thought. It was hard to understand how he knew, but there was a way about Aruna and, her eyes, that left subtle hints. Aruna was trying to appear happy, but between the bright sparks of in her eyes, a something dark lingered.

Mangarmyr felt a twinge in his heart, he'd seen that same dwindling sparks in his own reflection whenever he went to drink by the lake. He studied Aruna. It was such a puzzle.

"I guess, from your perspective, I am new." Aruna looked up, her gaze focusing on the other pale orb Mangarmyr had seen shining brightly above them. "We run across the night sky, forever free from what we left behind."

"So, you and the other are spirits?"

"I don't know. I didn't even think I could come back. I thought the sky would be my home, but seeing you. When you spoke to me, something said I should go to you. So here I am."

"What of the other? Would they be mad you left your place?" Mangarmyr asked.

She giggled. "He argued, but he's protecting me. He's always protected me."

"He?" Aruna nodded. It was curious, but at least Mangarmyr was more certain that she was a she. "Aruna, what's a human?"

Aruna sat back, a slight smirk crossing her face. It was as if no one had ever asked her before. "A human is this, like you are a wolf."

"I am Garou," Mangarmyr replied matter-of-factly.

"Ah yes, wolf spirits. But you are bigger than the others."

"I have always been different," he replied somberly. "The others shun me because of it."

She frowned. "You've always been alone, haven't you?"

He nodded. "For an eternity, it seems."

She leaned in close, draping her right arm over him and pulling him to her side. "Well, now you aren't. I am here."

"Are you also a 'he'?"

She laughed. "No, I'm a girl, silly, Garou."

Silence followed, but Mangarmyr didn't mind. The fire, Aruna, and the moment were enough. A moment later, the rumbling of his stomach stole the moment.

Aruna laughed. "You must be hungry. It's been hours since you've eaten." She stood, walking over to a gathering of trees. Mangarmyr noted a pair of moose antlers poking out from behind one of the pines.

How did I miss that? He thought as his eyes followed the antlers to the rest of the beast.

"I had to hide it with my magic," she commented. "I didn't want anyone else taking it."

"You killed it?"

"Why do you sound so surprised?"

"Well... you have no claws or fangs. You are very lean and do not seem suited for hunting."

Again she laughed. "Oh silly wolf," Aruna replied as she took the moose by the antlers and drug it closer to the fire. "I am more than human now."

"That is not a spirit," he commented.

She nodded. "No, it isn't. I have brought you to the real world."

"The 'real' world?"

"Some of you haven't learned how broken El'Anthar is yet," she answered somberly. "Here, things are much different from in The Veil. That is what the other spirits call your home now."

Mangarmyr sniffed at the moose's carcass. "When did this happen?"

"I don't know when," Aruna answered, pulling a strange object from beneath her clothes. It had a sheen to it and ended at a narrow point.

Mangarmyr had seen stones with a similar shape. They could cut you easily enough with their jagged edges. This object, however, wasn't made of any stone he had seen.

"It's called a knife," Aruna explained. "Humans use them for different things. Since we don't have claws, we have to make them from the earth."

"How strange," Mangarmyr commented as she used the 'knife' to cut into the moose. "So, will you eat the parts you cut off?"

"Eventually, but I have to cook it first," she replied. "Though I don't really need to eat anymore. I do it because I want to."

While curious about what she meant by 'cook', Mangarmyr was more interested in what she had meant by not having to eat. "What happened to you?"

Aruna stopped, planted the knife in the moose's side, and with a wave of her hand, caused the blood on her to vanish. "We were rescued, my brother and I. We were different from our own kind, just like you. So different, in fact, that it drew the attention of a powerful demon. A demon who wanted our power for himself."

Her eyes drifted to the snow at her feet. "Aruna, you don't have to tell me if it's too painful." She nodded and turned her attention back to the moose.

Mangarmyr watched her 'clean' the carcass. She divided up portions of it for herself and for him. Though it was strange why she would put her portions over the fire, but the aroma it gave off was appealing. The flavor of the meat differed from the moose he hunted in The Veil.

While spirits were forbidden from eating their own kind, they could hunt those who were prey according to The Cycle.

"Did you mean what you said?" he asked. "That I have you now?"

She smiled warmly. "I did. It's not good to be alone, so whether I'm here or up there, I will always be watching you."

Mangarmyr tilted his head. "Are you saying you will be my mate?"

She wore an odd expression, though it was hard to understand. Her face turned red at first, before breaking into a smile. Then she laughed.

"I'm saying I will be your friend, silly Garou."

"Is a friend like having a pack?"

She drew closer, wrapping her arms around him. "Yes, something like that. We will be a pack, you and I."

Mangarmyr leaned into her, nearly knocking Aruna off balance with his size. "Then, we will be a pack," he said matter-of-factly. His heart, however, was racing. Excitement washed over him. After so long, he had formed a pack.

He rose, seeing for the first time how much larger he was than Aruna. Her head barely met with his shoulder, leaving Mangarmyr towering towered over her. "Then, as a pack, we should hunt and make a den."

"But we just ate."

"We have, but I need to show you our domain so we can protect it together. Then we need a den, so when our pack grows, they will have a place to rest."

He lowered himself, allowing her to climb onto his back. She seemed uncertain at first, but took her time and climbed up. Mangarmyr stood, catching her somber expression from the corner of his eye. Something was wrong.

"I have to go," she said. "My brother is calling me. I have been away too long."

"But we are a pack. We stay together."

Aruna gently run her fingers through the thick fur between Mangarmyr's ears. "We will be. Whether down here or I'm up there. I will always be with you. Distance won't matter."

Mangarmyr bowed his head. Instinct told him she had her place in The Cycle too. It would be selfish to ask her to defy it. Though, just this once, part of him wanted her to.

"Close your eyes. I need to take you home," she said.

Mangarmyr did as she asked. A moment later, like water passing over him, he felt as if someone had dunked him in a lake. When the sensation passed, he opened his eyes and immediately could tell that he was indeed home. The world was brighter. Its colors fuller and alluring. Even the air was fresher.

"Why is the other place so dull?" he asked. But when he craned his neck to look back at her, Aruna was gone. Mangarmyr looked at the night sky. It was fading. Dawn would come soon. He Glimpsed Aruna, hiding behind her brother, but there was a sense that she was indeed watching.

Inwardly, he smiled. *While it was brief, I pray Adoshen grants us another meeting, Aruna.*

— Asger —

Asger gently ran his fingers through the dire wolf's fur. "Old man Garm is always ranting about the spirits. So they're real?"

Brandt shrugged. "Who knows? But only a fool dismisses what he doesn't understand."

"So Mangarmyr met Aruna. It seems odd for someone to be so open with a stranger."

"Well, boy, the spirits differ from us. They're more honest and have nothing to hide. Supposedly, they are an aspect of the natural world."

Asger eyed the older man thoughtfully. "You think the druids know about them?"

Again Brandt shrugged. "I've never heard anyone from Yggsid speak about them. Even Lalonna has never mentioned them."

Asger pursed his lip. Lalonna was a druid that came to the village from Yggsid a few years ago. She was Shaylin and never spoke of her age, so it was hard to know just how old she was.

"Maybe I should ask her?"

"Doubt you'd get an answer even if she knew. Them druids can be a bit tight-lipped."

Asger laughed. "You're only saying that because she rejected your advances."

"Hey, boy, now listen. If she's old enough to be on her own, then she's gotta be at least three hundred winters. Plenty old enough for me."

"Old enough to be your gran, and then some," Asger teased.

Brandt snickered, then burst out laughing. "Probably so, but she doesn't look a day out of her twenties."

Asger shook his head. "So, the story. What happened to Mangarmyr? How long was it before he and Aruna met again?"

"Not long. Though by our measure of time, who can what long for a spirit is?"

– Mangarmyr –

The cold air burned his lungs, but he had to keep running. The Fenrir were closing and the terrain offered no advantage. Mangarmyr stole a glance at the night sky. Aruna was hiding behind her brother.

I can feel you watching! We're supposed to be a pack... Help me!

The howls of the Fallen drew close. They were moving to corner him. Since his defeat of the other three, more Fenrir had come to challenge him. They sought power. His power.

In the days since the first attack, Mangarmyr had slain and purified dozens of Fenrir. Not just Fenrir, though. A Barzrine, an Urasen or fallen bear spirit, had come as well. The brute was thankfully stupid and easily deceived, which made purifying it easy.

A series of howls came from his right and Mangarmyr stopped, his momentum carrying him slightly forward in the snow. *They've already surrounded me!*

He focused his power, altering his form. His front paws became hands, similar to Aruna's, but covered with fur and ending in sharp claws. His body changed as well, giving him the ability to walk upright, but only for short distances.

Moving felt awkward, and by the look of himself, Mangarmyr knew he should have heeded his mother's advice. *You were right mother, I should have practiced this magic more.*

Taking to the trees, he climbed up the nearest pine and began dashing through the branches. Under his weight, some nearly gave, almost causing Mangarmyr to lose his balance. He focused more. Trying to image a form similar to Aruna's. To the Garou's surprise, his body responded. Though he looked more like somewhere between what she was and a wolf.

More howls echoed in the distance, forcing him to move. Mangarmyr climbed higher, surprised how much easier it was to move in his new form. He could leap further and grasp the branches more easily. Balancing on the branches was less awkward.

As he moved through the trees, it was clear his pursuers wouldn't relent. They were determined to devour him, and possibly each other afterward. Fenrir packs were unstable and self serving. The strongest ruled with a will of iron, but was on constant alert for betrayal.

Catching his breath, Mangarmyr knew he would have to fight. There were at least eight Fenrir and there was enough shadow for them to lie in wait for an ambush. He dropped to the ground, again surprised how easily his body moved.

Crouching low, he buried his hands in the snow, forcing his power into the ground. Like before, he infused his power into the powder to create the trap. Should any Fenrir step out in to the open, the snow would harden and impale them instantly. He then moved on to the trees.

Wherever the snow touched, his power found a foothold. The effort was exhausting, and he felt control over his new form slipping. Once he finished, Mangarmyr crouched low to the ground.

Now we wait. He cast his gaze to the sky. Aruna was still there. *Why can't you come down?*

"Tired of running, little cub?" the speaker's voice was full of contempt. By the way he spoke, the Fenrir addressing him was the Alpha.

Mangarmyr swept his eyes across the forest. Only darkness and shadow greeted him, despite the light given off by Aruna and her brother. Their glow seemed diminished, however. Not surprising, considering Fenrir could manipulate any place where there was shadow.

Mangarmyr checked the air. The sickening scent of the pack's taint blanketed the area, making it impossible to pinpoint their positioning. A chilling wind blew, further adding to the tension and silence.

Nervously, Mangarmyr shifted his weight. His heart raced as he scanned every dark crevice and mote of gloom around him. An attack could come from anywhere and without warming.

A pain yelp sounded to Mangarmyr's right as one of the trees he'd enchanted exploded in a hail of ice shards. He dropped to the ground to avoid getting caught in the spray of ice, bark, and wooden splinters.

"Kill him..." the pack leader commanded angrily.

Four Fenrir leaped from the darkness, parting from it like ghosts. Moments later, the snow around Mangarmyr erupted, becoming a sea of icy spikes, impaling them.

That's five.

The shadows deepened, becoming a black mist as it reached for him. Mangarmyr drew inward, focusing his breath and exhaling. Frost flowed from his mouth, carried by his breath, meeting the shadows head on. Upon contact, the inky black cloud melted away, its power dispelled.

Taking control of the frosted cloud, Mangarmyr shaped it into a bubble, halting the miasma's approach. As if to taunt him, three pairs of eyes greeted the Garou, their red glow shining through the black fog.

"How long can you maintain that?" the pack leader mused. "Until dawn? Do you think you can last that long?"

If only I could. Fenrir hated the sun. It weakened them. At night was when they or away from its light, was when they were at their strongest.

"No matter, wear yourself out. We will feed, growing stronger as you grow weaker."

Mangarmyr tried drowning out the sound of them feeding on their own, but it did little good. The Fenrir were blatantly taunting him. He dropped to one knee, fatigue taking hold. The Garou entertained the idea of pushing the barrier further out, but it was risky. His strength was already waning from maintaining it. Just hitting one of the Fenrir would be sheer luck, a gamble that would leave him open and exposed.

Aruna... You said we were a pack...

"Do I sense hopelessness, Garou?" The pack leader sniped. "You could always join us." A large charge chunk of flesh plopped near the edge of the barrier. It looked to be what was left of a hind quarter. The blood soaked into the snow, dissolving as it came in contact with the edge of the frosty barrier. "Feed and grow strong. What is it you fight for? Balance? The Cycle? Rubbish all of it."

"There is truth is darkness, Garou. You hunt Okashen instead of embracing them. You feed on them to purify your domain, yet why?" The miasma parted, and Mangarmyr saw his enemy. The Fenrir was as large as he, dwarfing his packmates beside him.

The spines on its back were curved, ending it barbs at their tips. The darkness moved about him like water, but clung to him like a mantle or cloak. A third eye sat at the center of his forehead, just under the single horn above it. This Fenrir was old and had probably fed on hundreds of spirits.

"I embraced the Okashen, took them into me and gained their power. I fell because I chose to. Adoshen lied, Garou. He has abandoned us, so rather than maintain this farce of balance and keeping the world as he intended, I shall master it and shape it to my will."

"I live to fulfill my purpose in this Cycle. Like those who came before me and as I have done in Cycles previous," Mangarmyr snapped. "I am part of it and will be so forever."

The pack leader sneered. "I will break you," he announced. The pair with him growled in protest.

"You promised us food and power. Yet you bargain?!"

Before its mouth closed, the miasma struck like a deadly blade, sweeping across the Fenrir's neck, decapitating him. The other lunged for the pack leader's throat, and was cut to pieces in an instant, its blood spraying onto the larger Fenrir's coat.

"Nuisances," the pack leader snarled. "Useless and stupid, both of them."

"Seems like such is my fate if I were to join you."

"No, little cub. You are different. You have so many of us, proving that though you lack the power of an Eldest, your cunning is in no short supply. In one fell swoop, you killed many of my packmates. It was an effortless play on our nature. You knew some would refuse to wait and one did. The others simply followed my command, revealing your trap."

"So you kept two in reserve, just to see what else I would do?"

The pack leader nodded. "See, clever. Clever is good. Clever is useful to me."

Mangarmyr winced. His stamina was giving out as the frosty barrier wavered. His form shifted, his appearance returning to normal. Desperate, he infused the last of his power into the surrounding snow, but the old Fenrir simply laughed.

"So that's your answer," he commented as the barrier gave. "Shame, then you'll just have to become part of me."

He stepped closer, triggering the effect of Mangarmyr's magic. The ice shards did nothing, however. The moment they touched the darkness cloaking the pack leader, they crumbled to dust. Mangarmyr collapsed in exhaustion, helpless to do anything as the miasma closed in. But as it was upon it, the black cloud shrank back.

"I just had a marvelous idea, Garou. What if I forced my packmates" blood down your throat? What if I made you eat their flesh?"

"I'll destroy you," Mangarmyr panted.

The Fenrir laughed, his third eyes taking on an ominous glow. "Once I turn you, Garou, you are welcome to try."

Mangarmyr look up at the night sky for what he thought would be the last time as himself. His heart lept, though he was uncertain why after seeing Aruna wasn't above them with her brother. She had no claws or fangs. What could she do against such a powerful enemy?

A low growl sounded behind the Fenrir. He paused, craning his neck behind him as a soft light illuminated the area. The miasma and the surrounding darkness dissolved and even he cowered, lowering his head as if in pain.

"Leave him alone!" Aruna commanded.

Slowly, the Fenrir backed away and Mangarmyr weakly raised his head. He could only stare at the white wolf bathing the area in its pale light. She was beautiful.

"My name is Hatisven, little cub. We will meet again." Hatisven bounded off and when he reached the limits of Aruna's light, melded into the darkness and vanished.

Aruna rushed to Mangarmyr's side, turning back into a human once she was close enough. "I'm so sorry, Mangarmyr! I wanted to come, but Eske wouldn't let me."

She was tears as she placed his large head in her lap. Mangarmyr closed his eyes, too tired to say anything. Aruna stroked his fur, tears still running down her cheeks.

"Why?" he finally asked. "Why did he stop you?"

"There are rules," she said, wiping her cheeks. "We can only watch the world, filling the night with our light. We cannot interfere. If we do, there will be consequences."

"What consequences?"

"I don't know. Neither does Eske, but Sharina warned us. I can leave the night sky only so often. Eske must stay there always. It was the price for her rescuing us long ago."

"How long can you stay?" Mangarmyr asked.

"Until dawn. I will stay with you until dawn."

Mangarmyr closed his eyes. "I'd like that," he replied.

She leaned forward, kissing him on the nose. "We are a pack."

Inwardly, Mangarmyr smiled. "Yes, Aruna, we are."

– Asger –

"So it seems like Mangarmyr's success in defending his home only got him into more trouble."

"In a way, but think about it," Brandt replied. "Can't the same be said for us and the Norens?"

Asger shrugged. "Well, our Riders do force them to bring their dragons."

Brandt nodded. "In war, one side is always trying to gain an advantage over the other. The frost giants raid us for different reasons, but ultimately their clans are convinced Sokoras belongs to them. The more successful we are in defending our homes, the more determined they are to subjugate us."

"Or cook us," Asger replied wryly.

"Those are only rumors, boy. The giants don't actually eat humans. That's just something for moder told you to keep you from acting up."

Asger shrugged. "So Aruna could become a wolf?"

"She could do a lot of things, Asger. She could have erased Hatisven on the spot for example, but as the story says, there were rules."

"What do you mean?"

"Honestly, I don't know. I've often wondered, but I think it goes along with The Cycle. Like, you know how if push the wolves too hard or fight them when they don't want to do something, they'll bite you, maybe even kill you?"

Asger nodded. "It's a relationship. Your wolf is your partner."

"And if you break the relationship and hurt the bond, nothing is ever the same, is it?"

"No, there's a rift."

"I think that's what she meant. Whatever her place in The Cycle, regardless of how powerful she may be, Aruna could do only so much. She's connected to something we may not understand, but works as was intended."

Asger turned to the fire in the hearth, his eyes growing heavy. *It must be close to the night's midden by now,* he thought. The cold was a bit much with a storm on the horizon, so Brandt offered the warmth of a fire and a stiff drink to ward off the cold.

"Should we call it a night?" Brandt asked.

He shook his head. "No, keep going. It's not like there's anything good waiting for me at home. Da's prolly passed out on the floor again."

"He wasn't always like that, you know," Brandt offered.

"So you keep telling me."

The dour look on Brandt's face sad it all. Asger felt a little guilty for sounding so harsh. "I'm sorry, uncle."

"Things are what they are, Asger. Coating it with niceties won't change that."

"So what happened next?"

Brandt took a sip of mead from his mug. "Aruna and Mangarmyr got close. She spent many nights with him, sometimes riding on his back or as a wolf. They even hunted together. Though whenever she hunted with him, it wasn't in spirit realm."

"But, the more time she spent with him, the less time she spent in the night sky."

– **Mangarmyr** –

While the days were quiet, the nights were full of bliss. Mangarmyr felt his heart beat faster the lower the sun set on the horizon. From the entrance to the cavern, he watched the shows grow longer with every moment. After Hatisven ran off, no more Fenrir dared enter his domain. It was a relief, leaving him to hunt Okashen and other spirits as according to the Cycle.

Mangarmyr looked about the cavern. Aruna had helped him find it. It made for a good den and a place to rest.

Now I just need a mate. He thought of Aruna, his heart fluttering. To himself, he knew she couldn't be. She wasn't Garou, and she was the moon, far from his reach with her own responsibilities.

A shadow cast itself on the entrance, and Mangarmyr turned his mind to the present. It was hard to see against the rays of sunlight pushing past the person standing at the cave opening. The Garou squinted, his heart sinking when he realized it wasn't Aruna.

"Leave my sister alone," a hard male voice warned. "Aruna has her place, and it is not with you."

Mangarmyr stood, hackles raised. "She is my pack. She does as she pleases and you will not tell me what I cannot do."

Something suddenly forced the air from his lungs, and Mangarmyr gagged, struggling for breath. "Know your place dog, you too small to understand the scope of what is happening around you."

"Then I will return you to The Cycle, so you are but a memory."

Mangarmyr reached deep, but lack of air stole his focus. He couldn't muster the strength to use his magic. As his vision blurred, the shadows of sunset grew longer still, until, at the last moment, Eske's hold over him suddenly loosed.

He wheezed, coughing, and fighting to regain his breath. Looking up, he realized what had happened. The sun had set, forcing Aruna's brother to take his place in the heavens.

Weakly, he rose, plodding toward the mouth of the cave. Standing there to greet him just a few paces from the entrance was Aruna. She had chosen to be a wolf tonight. Putting what had happened behind him, Mangarmyr rushed to her, stroking his muzzle against hers.

"What's gotten into you?" she asked.

"I just missed you," he replied. "You are my light in the night."

Silence followed as she rested her forehead against his. "I missed you too." Aruna walked toward the cave entrance, then stopped, lifting her head toward the sky. "I cannot stay tonight. Sharina is angry."

"What does that mean?"

"I have broken the Cycle..."

He ran to her, shifting his form so he could wrap his arms around her. She, in turn, became human, to hold him back properly. "How?"

"I have visited you too much. Even on nights when I was supposed to remain by my brother's side. I have killed many Fenrir, burned them with my light to keep you safe. Now I fear something is coming to take their place, to rebalance The Cycle."

Mangarmyr sat with her in silence. He studied her form and drew on his power even more. To his surprise, he became as close to a human as he could. His ears longer and pointed, with tufts of fur at their edges.

His fingers ended in claws, and fur covered his arms and chest. At the base of his spine sat a bushy tail.

"I don't think I can go any further," he explained. "But I can try."

She smiled warmly, gently caressing his cheek. "This is enough." Her hand took on a soft white glow and Aruna touched his chest. A white robe took shape around him, but after looking at Mangarmyr, she burst into laughter.

"What?" he asked, frowning as he adjusted the robe. "It feels strange."

"Just you," she replied with a smile and rested her head against his chest.

"Aruna..."

"Shh... Don't speak."

Mangarmyr complied, content to just hold her. He sensed tiny hints of Aruna's emotions. Her sadness and worry. Her fears and yearnings for things to be different. It didn't seem fair.

Do you see now, little cub?

Mangarmyr tensed. Hatisven? A sense of amusement washed over him.

I've been watching you, Mangarmyr. You and your moon. What would you do to keep her? The Cycle you laud so faithfully betrays you.

We all have our part to play, Fenrir. Even you...

Oh? He replied. Do I now? Then what part of this ridiculous fantasy do I play?

The Cyle is about balance; you are dark to the light.

The Fenrir's laughter rang out in his mind. *How utterly stupid. I am free of such trappings. I broke your Cycle, so I can live as I wish! Perhaps I should take your precious moon away and prove it to you.*

I will kill you if you try, Mangarmyr cut back.

You know my answer, little cub. Come and try.

"Mangarmyr..." Aruna gasped. "You're hurting me."

Mangarmyr froze. He'd been crushing Aruna in an iron embrace. "I'm sorry. I was lost in thought."

"My brother came to visit, didn't he?"

The wolf spirit nodded. "He threatened to return me to The Cycle if I didn't stay away."

Her eyes flashed in anger. "He will not!"

The air suddenly became electric, giving Mangarmyr a hint of how powerful she really was. "Aruna... how did you break the cycle?"

"I shine to give others hope. I only appear in the night sky for those who need to see me. It is hard to explain. While Eske shines for everyone, I shine for a small few. Even when in the sky, few see me. I'm always hidden behind him, catching a view of our world in mere glimpses."

"So you're a prisoner…"

"No, I serve a purpose. Had Sharina not saved us, we would be the slaves of a demon. Tools to grow his power and hurt others. Now we use our power to add to the world. Go give light and hope. Our light can heal and protect."

"So when you are with me, you neglect the world?"

She nodded somberly. "I can't be a guide if I'm not there to look down on those who need me."

"So when you saw me, I was like the others?"

"No, you were more. You stood out, even in The Veil. I saw you and couldn't stop staring. When you almost died, laying in the snow alone and broken… I couldn't leave you. Just helping you so directly violated The Cycle."

"Do you regret helping me?" even as the words left his lips, Mangarmyr felt a twinge of guilt for asking. It was obviously stupid to voice such thoughts, but part of him needed to know.

"No, not once," she replied, then pulled away. He shifted back, giving her room. "I have to go, Mangarmyr. Sharina is calling me. Her patience has run out."

"Will I see you again?"

Aruna smiled, a tear running down her cheek. "You will always see me. I'll be looking down at you from above. Even if we can't speak, I'm still here."

She vanished seconds later, leaving the Garou alone at the cave entrance. Mangarmyr's chest tightened. The anguish in his heart was too great to bear. And as he raised his head to the night sky, a long mournful howl escaped his throat.

The cry was so great that without knowing what he had done; he infused his magic into the sound. Creatures for miles could hear it, each frozen in their tracks. None had ever heard anything like it and soon after, other Garou came to investigate. Others, so overcome with the sense of grief in Mangarmyr's howl that they too called out to the night sky.

It became a chorus of such power that all the Fenrir in the region ran for their lives. All except for Hatisven. He was more than pleased to use Mangarmyr's grief to his advantage.

– Asger –

"Is all of this actually true, Uncle?"

The old wolf rider smiled. "It's a myth, Asger, you tell me. I'm just sharing what your granmoder told me. It's one of a few stories she would tell when I was your age."

"So I assume that's why wolves howl at the moon?"

"No, and yes."

"The story's not done?"

Brandt frowned. "Bored already?"

Asger shook his head. "No, I'm very curious. Though I'm thinking this is just some drunken fable you cooked up."

"Now, listen here, boy. I'm far from drunk and this is a story passed down for several generations! It's your heritage!"

Asger snickered, though admittedly he'd drunk a bit more than Brandt, so his uncle's expression shouldn't have been nearly as funny as it was. "You should see your face." He always took family heritage seriously.

Brandt scowled. "You say that now, but when you have a boy of your own, you will be tellin' it to him all the same."

"Sure, uncle, I'll find the time between tending the wolves."

Brandt laughed. "You'll see."

Asger shrugged. "Maybe. So, did Mangarmyr ever see her again?"

"Not for many years. But he never stopped loving her," Brandt replied. "But a curious happened during that time."

"Oh?"

"His mournful cry drew the attention of other Garou. Some ventured into Mangarmyr's territory. A few of them female."

Asger eyed his uncle curiously. "So he found a mate?"

Brandt laughed. "No, boy. You don't fall in love just to give up at the first sigh of trouble! You fight for it!"

"So, all those years alone and he finally has an opportunity to take a mate and he gives it up?"

"Because none of them were her, Asger. In his heart Mangarmyr has chosen his mate long before he even realized it. So no matter who came calling, no matter how beautiful they were, none could compare to Aruna. The Garou may have have suddenly looked at him differently, but without Aruna, none of it mattered."

"It's ironic isn't it? To long for soemthing so long only to cast it aside when you finally get it."

"Aye, it is. But that when you know what you were after wasn't real. It was only the power covering up what lay beneath. All mangarmyr ever wanted was a connection. Someone to end his longstanding lonliness."

Asger drew his lips taut. "It's tragic."

"It's life," his ungle replied. "Even the spirits sometimes confuse what they want with what they need. In the end, we all need that one connection to be the stake that keeps our tent moored and sturdy."

Asger nodded. "I imagine that on the nights when she wasn't in the sky, he hoped Aruna would come visit."

"You would right. He hoped beyond reason and would even howl at Eske as if pleading with him to let his sister visit him. But she never came. Aruna had to fulfill her responsibilities to the world."

"Why do I feel like Hatisven was waiting to take advantage?"

"Because you're a smart kid," Brandt answered. "Hatisven was watching and eager to turn Mangarmyr into a Fenrir."

— Mangarmyr —

"Still sulking, little cub?" Hatisven asked.

Mangarmyr sneered. "You come every day, just to taunt me…"

In his own way the old Fenrir gave Mangarmyr the impression he was smiling. "Can't I check on someone I'm concerned about?"

Mangarmyr chuffled. "Concern?" he replied. "I know sunk to new depths if a Fenrir is concerned about my well being."

Hatisven laughed, so hard in fact that he fell to the ground, paws covering his muzzle as he rolled back and forth in amusement. "Oh, Mangarmyr, this is why I like you. I haven't laughed like that in ages. Your sour demeanor is like a breath of fresh air."

"You just want another pawn. A servant to exploit."

"Perhaps, but at least more honest than your precious moon."

Mangarmyr whipped around snapping his jaws mere inchest from the Fenrir's muzzle. "Watch your tone!"

As if pleased with himself, the old Fenrir circled behind Mangarmyr. "I will never lie to you, Mangarmyr. My intentions will always be true. Even if I were to betray you, would that such a surprise?"

Mangamyr looked away. "No. I would expect nothing less."

"See, that the beauty of being in a pack with me. No secrets, little cub. I wil laways be true to my nature and as long as you remain useful, I will never have a need to be rid of you."

"The Cycle..."

"To Shundule with The Cycle!" the old Fenrir snapped. The shadows around him deepened, moving as if alive. "You continue to play this game with no benefit. A slave t oa system that niether wants you nor care you live or die. You simple exist to serve a meaninless purpose all in the name of 'balance'. But whose balance and why?!"

Mangarmyr grew quiet. Then after Hatsiven calmed down, spoke. "Without balance our world dies. It breaks and everyoen suffers."

"Our world is dying you fool! It is broken and all are suffering! Rather than be the victim of it, take control. Be its master and shape it as you see fit. Do not remain as some servant of a corpse that doesn't know when to lie down!"

Mangarmyr stepped away from him, turning his attention to the pines all around them. *How is the world dying?*

"Come with me." Hatisven's tone was strange, it wasn't an invitation, but niether a command, but soemwhere in between.

"Why?"

"To show you the truth," the old Fenrir replied.

That shadows around him thicknt, then swirled, forming an opening similar to a cave. He stepped through, the darkness swallowing him. Mangarmyr took step closer to the shadowy gateway, then hesitated.

Either live in ignorance and die a slow death or see the truth and be set free, Mangarmyr heard in his mind.

Stealing away his fear, Mangarmyr stepped through the portal and when he came out on the other side, his heart nearly stopped. Before lay a horrific landscape. Trees lay wtihered and appearing dead, yet he could sense they were soemhow still alive.

The earth was black as if burned, but also soft like clay. Some of it bubbled, like water boiling in a lake. The spirits he could see, both elemental and animal were grim, sickly mockeries of their former selves. A few were ones he knew, Fallen that found the sickly spirits easy prey.

Only by feeding on those weaker than themselves were the yrestored to some semblence of who they had once been. It a mockery of The Cycle, everything consuming another, but without anything being purfied and restored.

"Welcome to the Blighted Lands," Hatisven announced. As if to accent his ominous tone, thunder roared above them. A storm was coming. Mangarmyr saw lighting dancing between thick black clouds and within them, more spirts danced, each attacking the other, consuming and consumed.

"What is this..."

"This is the work of mortals," Hatisven replied as if that were supposed to have some meaning. "Come," he said.

The world around warped momentarily. The landscape shifted and immediately Magarmyr knew they were in the physical world. The lanscape was desolate, wit hfew trees and only sparse clumps of grass. The ground was brittle and dry and though rain began falling from the sky, it felt as if it lacked the nourishment the earth needed.

"Here is the truth. Here is the wound that will destroy everything."

Mangarmyr balked. "But how?"

"Demons," he answered matter-of-factly. "When I saw this, I knew my purpose was pointless. This wound will grow and fester. The fate of the spirits here will be the fate of all. So chose to take control of my destiny. If I cannot defeat it, then I will help it and become powerful enough to avoid the fate of those weaker than myself. I will consume, not be consumed."

Mangarmyr backed away. "No, there is a way."

The shadows around the Fenrir shifted, dancing around him like serpents poised to strike. He craned his neck over his shoulder, red eyes glowing brightly in the night. "Surely you are not this stupid? Even in the face of the inevitable?"

"These mortals, are there none who appose what they have done?"

The Fenrir laughed. "I don't care even if there are. My only concern is surviving this. I chose you becaue you aren't like other Garou. You aren't weak, you don't deserve to be prey, unless it is my prey."

A chill ran down Mangarmyr's spine. "Why me? I'm just Garou."

"You are ignorant aren't you?" His tone was full of utter disbeleif.

"Do you not know, how powerful you really are?! Have you not considered how long you have lived? Even I can sense it."

Mangarmyr shook his head.

"How many Garou can shange their shape as you have? How many have you seen?"

Mangarmyr paused. "None."

"Even as you say that, you answer as if you expected all of you were so capable. But you are wrong. You have been alone this entire time not because you are so powerful. The other Garou sense it and fear it."

"But I am just Garou. Born like any other."

"Have you ever thought about what happens to an Eldest when they die. If they die?"

Mangarmyr froze. *All spirits return to The Cycle... Even the Eldest.*

"Now you understand. That power simply doesn't fade. It is part of you. You are an Eldest reborn you fool. You may not remember your life before or all of who you were, but your power is the same."

"How do you know this?" Mangarmyr asked.

The old Fenrir's red eyes took on a feral glint. "Because I am an Eldest. I chose to become Fenrir. I am The Fenrir. I remember you Skolander, even if you do not remember yourself. I will never forget the power of your spirit. It's like your paw print in the snow."

As if you prove he wasn't lying. Hatisven doubled in size. A two more heads sprouted beside the first as the shadows danced about his paws like living flames. The spines on his back thickened, becoming like horns. The third eye on his center head gave off a pale green glow and Mangarmyr found himself unable to look away from it.

The bushy tail Hatisven once had lengthened, the fur on it falling away as long barbs overtook its scaly surface. He looked more demonic than Mangarmyr could have imagined, leaving the Garou frozen in place. His power was undeniable, however.

"See now why I never fear you harming me, little cub. For what can a lion that thinks he's a mere flea possibly accomplish?"

"If I am an Eldest reborn, then I can stop you."

"Stop me?! Stop me?" Hatisven laughed. "Skolander, let me show you how powerless you are." The world warped and Mangarmyr found himself standing outside a strange mountain covered in lights. There was nothing natural about its spires and towers. The stonework looked manufactered, like the places sacred to the Old Ones.

"This is what mortals call a 'city'. They wall thesmelves up behind a stone barrier to protect against the horrors of this world. They use magic to try and keep safe, but it is useless."

"What are you going to do?"

"I'm going to kill them all. I will devour their souls and leave this city a pile of ash. If after I finish, you still refuse to join me, Skollander, then I will consume you next. But if you join me, I will show you how to rightly use your power and become a proper Eldest."

"I will no..."

"Shhh... just watch before you answer foolishly." Th Fenrir turned his back, bounding toward the 'city'. As Hatisven closed in on the walls, the darkness surrounding him thickened, moving like a mist or fog. The miasma rushed ahead of him, swelling in size like a raging tempest. The barrier around the city crumbled at its touch and Hatisven disappeared into the murk.

Screams followed next as fiery bursts flashed within the black fog. The on wind, the smell of sulfur and blood drifted in on the stagnant air. More screams flowed in the night, each differing in pitch and tone, like a macabre melody. Explosion rocked the city, its towers crumbling.

Mangarmyr stood frozen, his paws firmly planted in the barren grown. He could sense each death, piercing his heart. He looked to the sky and to his shock, Aruna's glow lacked its beautiful luster. Instead, she bore a crimson radiance as she peered from behind Eske.

I wish you were here, he thought. *Are you weeping for them too? Is this the darkness you spoke of?*

Hours passed as the slaughter continued, from the horizon, the subtle rays of dawn were beginning to grasp the mountains in the distance. Hatisven was running out of time. He'd be weakened in the day.

As the screams grew less frequent, the sun had pulled itself a little more over the horizon. The shadow and gloom of the night had begun its retreat. Even the black miasma covering the city had thinned.

Eventually, once the city had gone silent, Hatisven burst from the black fog, bounding closer to Mangarmyr. "It seems luck is with you, Skolander," he said, coming to a halt. "I will await your answer on tomorrow's eve. To not test my patience." Hatisven cloaked himself in shadow and when it parted, he was gone.

Mangarmyr gazed about the bleak dead landscape, then at the ruins of the city. His heart ached. Loneliness had taken root. Looking to the the horizon, the sun was almost free of the mountains. "What do I do now?" he whispered softly.

He looked to the sky. Eske and Aruna were nearly gone, the bright blue hues of the morning sky cloaking them. They were like ghosts. Just barely visible.

"Aruna…please come back." He nearly jumped when he felt someone take hold of him in a tender embrace.

"My precious Garou," Aruna said, tearfully.

Mangarmyr immidately transformed, taking her into his arms. They held he other tightly, their hearts overflowing with more emotion than they could express. So they cried, not just for the dead, but for each other. The distance between them had been like an ocean and now together, it was suddenly filling.

"I wanted to stop him, but I couldn't." she sobbed. "I wanted to save you, but they wouldn't let me."

"I love you Aruna. Before you I was alone. Without you I will always be alone."

She pulled back, gazing into his dark eyes. Shock shone on her face. "Mangarmyr… You look human," she gasped.

Mangarmyr paused, taking another look at himself. "Hatisven said I was an Eldest reborn. Can an Eldest do such things?"

She leaned in and kissed him tenderly. "The eldest can become many things. But they always choose a form dearest to their hearts."

Without thinking, he kissed her back, and they held each other, locked in a tender embrace. Aruna made clothes for him as a harsh wind blew in. Mangarmyr wanted to say something, anything, but words failed him. Eventually, he kissed her again and they gave into their passions, expressing themselves in ways words could not.

"Skollander..."

Mangarmyr looked up. Aruna was fading, her appearance becoming more like phantom or figment by the moment. Her time was up.

"I know," he said. "Aruna, are we a pack... or are you, my mate?"

"I will be your mate, forever and always," she whispered, kissing him one last time before fading away as the sun's rays fell on her. *I'll never abandon you again, my precious Garou. Even apart, part of you will be with me.*

Bolstered after she had spoken to his mind, Mangarmyr rose, clothing himself with the robes Aruna had made for him. "Now I just have to get home."

***

In the quiet of his den, Mangarmyr waited through the night. The silence was like a stone pressing into his chest, pushing sharply against his heart. He lifted his head from his paws, eyes fixated on the cave entrance. Hatisven, still hadn't shown.

In Eske's light, a shadow cast itself across the entrance. Mangarmyr tensed, narrowed his eyes as he stared at the opening. A moment later, Aruna appeared, her warm smile chasing his apprehension into the night.

"He's not coming," she announced as he ran to greet her.

Mangarmyr pressed his muzzle against her cheek and she, in turn, gently stroked it with her hands. "Why has he not come?" Aruna held him, her arms stretching his neck as she leaned into him. "Aruna?"

"What does it matter?" He pulled back, ears twitching. "Mangarmyr?"

"What did you do?" She turned away. "Aruna?"

"I warned him. If he comes near you, I will kill him. Not just kill him, erase him."

"You can't, will that not disrupt The Cycle further?"

"It doesn't matter now," she replied. "The Pendulum has shifted too far." She touched her belly. "Things are in motion to a greater degree than before."

She felt so distant. So empty. Though his love was close, she seemed so far away. "Aruna, what's wrong?"

She came closer, taking his muzzle into her hands and kissing him on the nose. "I love you, Mangarmyr."

Mangarmyr transformed and held her. "I love you too." The cave grew quiet, and they moved to sit on the smooth rocky floor, each holding the other.

Eske's light barely reached inside the entrance, but it was enough for them to see each other in his pale light. Mangarmyr leaned against the cold stone wall, a chill running up his bare back. Her eyes were closed, and he smiled, holding her tighter.

Aruna leaned into him, pressing her back against his chest. "I want this to last forever. I can feel your warmth. The kindness of your heart and the gentleness in your spirit," she said. "The world of men is so different from the spirit. There's so much deception and lies. So many things one has to shield themselves from. Honesty is foreign and feared... but so is love."

"Why? How can anyone live that way?"

"Look at Hatisven. He craves power and fears death. He fears an imagined reality, so he clings to what he can. Lying, killing, and taking along the way."

"But he is Fenrir, that is their nature." Her bottom lip drew taut as if she were upset. "Aruna?"

"Just hold me or kiss me," she said.

He pulled her against him, kissing her neck. She exhaled, reaching back, and grabbing his scalp. Then turning her head, her lips met his, before both became lost in the moment and let their desire consume them.

For several nights after, they met, casting their worries aside until Hatisven became a distant memory. Like they used, Aruna would become a wolf and let Mangarmyr chase her. Sometimes he would run from her, and she would have to catch him. At other times, they would slip between realms, visiting both the world of mortals and the spirit. But for each, being together mattered more than anything.

Aruna would teach him about mortals in their forays, both good and bad. Mangarmyr would tell her of his world, and even if she already knew, Aruna would simply listen. Her smile shining like a flare in the night.

Yet, as the days went on, Mangarmyr sensed a shadow looming over them. But if Aruna noticed it, she said nothing. Whether in the quiet moment or the passionate ones. Whether in their most intimate moments or most playful. Mangarmyr's heart was firmly entwined with hers.

As they watched the sun rise on the horizon, Mangarmyr's heart felt heavy. "I hate seeing you leave."

"I know," she said, leaning into him and holding him. "But I have to. Sharina set the rules."

She bit her lip, a sign of frustration. "You have people to help, don't you?"

Aruna nodded. "I do. I've been watching them during the day. I can't come back for a while."

"I know…" he replied. "I've sensed it for some time now."

"It won't be forever. What is time to us?"

Mangarmyr half smiled. "Even a moment away from you is an eternity."

"You always make me smile," she said, then looked up, pulling him closer and kissing him.

"I will think of you."

"When are you not?" she teased.

Mangarmyr laughed. It wasn't like he could deny it. The sun climbed over the peaks to the east and, just like that, Aruna vanished with its rays.

***

Like so many nights before, Mangarmyr waited, his gaze locked on the cave entrance. Dyas became weeks, then months, then years. Sometimes he would gaze at the sky and there she would be, so close, yet so far away. Seeing her wasn't enough, but it still gave some comfort. He had to be content with that.

But one night, when he went to gaze at the sky, Aruna was gone. His heart leapt. *She's coming. She's finally coming back to me!*

Excited, he went inside his den, eyes fixated on the cave's entrance. Yet as the night went on, Aruna still hadn't shown. Disheartened, he stood and walked toward it, lifting his head to the heavens once he was outside.

"Mangarmyr?"

Mangarmyr turned, his heart racing after laying eyes on her. "I was worried."

She embraced him, her arms stretching around his neck. "I was delayed. One of those who needed me died."

Mangarmyr froze. "Aruna..."

"I'm okay," she said, trying to reassure him. "It's part of The Cycle. I'm not everyone's answer."

There was something in her tone. It lacked a level of compassion, as if Aruna she was forcing herself to feel something. Mangarmyr backed away, toward the cave's entrance. "Who are you?"

'Aruna' grinned, her teeth turning into sharp canines. "Aww, young pup, am I not enough?"

Mangarmyr snarled. "Where is she?!"

"Who can say?" Hatisven replied. "But you'll never see her again."

The temperature in the chamber dropped sharply. Ice crystals spread like wildfire from Mangarmyr's paws, flash freezing everything. The ice, however, wove its way around the Fenrir, making a small circle.

"Good, now we're getting somewhere," he commented. Shifting to his true form, Hatisven drew closer. "Do you really think you can kill me, Skollander?"

"Stop calling me that!" Mangarmyr snapped. "That is not who I am now!"

"Clearly." The Fenrir's tone dripped with disappointment. "I supposed I should simply kill you. Maybe in your next life I can track you down and force you to see reason."

Mangarmyr created a barrier of ice between them. "What are you so obsessed with me?"

"Because, little brother, family should stay together. We were kings once, and we will be again."

Mangarmyr stared at him, eyes wide. "Brother?" Mangarmyr could sense the Fenrir's amusement. "When I lost you during the Second Dawn, after their corruption infecting our world. I had nothing left. There was so much death and rather than becoming prey, I chose to remain the hunter."

"You used to joke about catching the sun, that you would ascend to the heavens and hold it in your powerful jaws. I would laugh, of course. We weren't the kind of spirits whose reach extended that far. But you insisted, because it couldn't be done."

There were no words, but for some reason, Mangarmyr knew Hatisven spoke the true. It was like an itch, or a thought so vague that it remained out of reach. Yet Mangarmyr's heart quickened. He still had family.

"I can cleanse you," he offered. "Purify your essence."

Hatisven laughed. "And what, return me to your pitiful Cycle? To perpetuate the futility of our existence? No, little cub, I am far too gone for that, and I don't care anymore."

"But you won't die, we can still be family..."

Again the Fenrir laughed. "You idiot, do you think I care for family? I want your power, one way or another."

"If you didn't care so much, you would have killed me long ago."

A soft growl escaped Hatisven's throat. "Don't project your own weakness onto me!"

Like a thunderbolt, his words cut deep. The thought was a memory. Mangarmyr felt it nearly within reach of his paw. He strained for it, pushing to grasp it, yet it slipped through.

"Don't ignore me! You always did that!"

Mangarmyr just barely heard him. Yet again, Hatisven's words struck a cord. The memory, like a thin thread, was so close. *Don't ignore me!*

The phrase was so simple, but as deep as one of the great lakes. *Don't ignore me...* Then it came flooding back. The battle, Hatisven's pleas to run, instead of fighting alongside the Adenshar, Father's children. All the time they had spent together since first waking.

Hatisven always preferred the night. He would lie around all day unless roused from his sleep. He hunted drakes with the E'nstar, the dragon spirits, gazed at the stars, always wondering why the sun stood alone and pondered The Cycle often.

Movement barely registered before Mangarmyr had time to react. Hatisven had lunged toward him. He ducked low, craning his neck to catch his younger brother by the throat, and slung him against the cave wall.

Hatisven stood, shock spreading across his face. "You remember," he whispered, as if recalling a fight they had once before.

"Leave, little brother." Mangarmyr commanded. "I remember who was the eldest and who won our fights."

"Things are different now, Skollander. I'm not as weak as I was then."

"It doesn't matter," he said, his tone of voice becoming all too familiar. "I have what I want, for now." He sounded like Aruna.

"What have you done?"

"I have a trophy. Do as I say and she may live. I wonder what would happen to the world if it lost one of its precious moons?" Before he could react, Hatisven took advantage of the gloom and vanished.

Lost in a storm of emotions, Mangarmyr howled. Between the memories of who his brother was, who he is now, and the fear of losing the one thing he loved most, Mangarmyr lost all strength and collapsed.

"Wait, my love, I'm coming. I know who I am now and what must be done."

— Asger —

So he was an Eldest the entire time..." Asger commented.

Brandt nodded. "A powerful one, too. The Eldest were born as creation, each had a purpose and role to fulfill. There were many, according to what your Gran told me."

"So what happened to Aruna? Obviously, she's still in the sky if the dire wolves can see her?"

"Suddenly you don't sound so skeptical of my story, boy." Brandt laughed and Asger frowned.

"It is interesting. That's all."

"Sure, boy." Brandt replied. "Sure"

His grin was annoying. "So... Mangarmyr or Skollander went hunting for Hatisven?"

"He did. With his memories awakened, Skollander could use the full extent of his powers. He could move between worlds. Ours and the spirit without help."

"But why didn't Eske step in? He came once before."

"Because, as Aruna said, there are rules," Brandt replied. "She had already sown the consequences of her actions."

"So, her being kidnapped was the dark thing that was to come?"

"No, Asger. It was something far worse."

– Mangarmyr –

He's searched everywhere, traveling through the mortal realms and the places where the spirits dwell. He's called out to Eske, screaming at him to come down and help, but Alrun'a brother silently hung in the sky. His light filled the night with its pale tones casting shadows among the pines and evergreens.

"No none of you care?!" Mangarmyr shouted. "How can you be so indifferent?!"

Silence greeted him. Along with the sound of the wind brushing between the trees. Mangarmyr howled in frustration. Grief had him in its grip.

"Now, now, dear spirit. Why don't you quiet down."

He spun on his paws, his eyes falling to a Fey-like female with long dark hair, sharp features and pointed ears. She reminded him of the Daenanelf, spirits decended of the Fey, but there was something off about her. She was much more powerful than any of the Fey he remembered.

She wore gown, with fabric that appeared woven from the night sky. It sparkled with tiny flares of strarlight as she moved closer. "Such a noisy creature."

Magarmyr tensed, crouching low as she approached. "Who are you?"

The 'Daenanelf' smiled. "Sharina," she replied. "Now, what do you want?"

"I want my mate back. I want Aruna."

"And you expect me to give her up?" Amusement stretched across her cheeks. "She was kidnapped, was she not?"

"So do something!"

"Oh, you expect me to do something?" She laughed, then waved her hand to the ground in front of her. A chair took shape from the earth and snow. "For an eldest, you are quite stupid," Sharina added dourly after seating herself.

"I remember everything from before, yet I still haven't regained all my strength. My body isn't the same as it was at the beginning."

"So, you understand your limitations?"

"And my sins..." he quickly added.

She titled her head thoughtfully. "Oh? Then, maybe we can restore balance."

Mangarmyr's ears perked up. "How?"

She smirked. "By waiting. The opportunity will arise, but requires patience. Act rashly and you will lose not only her, but everything else."

"What of the darkness Aruna mentioned?"

Her expression turned somber. "It grows by the day. It will find you soon enough."

She vanished before he could ask anything. Mangarmyr scanned the pines and gazed at the night sky. *Patience... Maybe if I hadn't met her, I could afford that luxury.*

***

The attacks were growing more frequent, but even in packs, the Fenrir seemed weaker than before. Yet despite how weak they were, the fallen spirits kept coming. Each night they grew in number and though he was able to rest during the day, Mangarmyr felt the toll.

Sleep left little time to hunt and replenish his strength. Loneliness made it even worse. It chipped at his heart, little by little. He winced, glancing at his shoulder. A Fenrir had managed to get a bite in. The wound was healing and not very deep, but it was one of the many annoyances robbing him of his sleep.

He raised his head, eyeing the cave entrance. The sun was retreating. *Maybe there's still time for food.*

Rising, he plodded toward the opening. Winter was almost here, the air was growing colder by the day. Closing his eyes, he slipped into the mortal realm. Most of the Fenrir would check the den before coming here.

Searching the countryside, Mangarmyr came across a moose. Inwardly, he smiled, his thoughts turning to the first night he'd met Aruna. Though when the moment passed, the longing returned. "It would be like that," he commented. "Well, maybe it's a sign."

He rushed the beast, pouncing on it, using his size and strength to topple it. The moose stumbled, turned, and lowered his head to charge. Mangarmyr planted his paws, tensing. The moose came at him, and he waited, clamping his powerful jaws down on the moose's left antler.

Turning with its momentum, he pulled the moose to the ground, turning its head at an awkward angle, until it lost balance and stumbled to the ground. Letting go, Mangarmyr attacked its front left leg, snapping it.

The moose cried out, flailing its head and slamming its horns into Mangarmyr's wounded left shoulder. He yelped, but fought through the pain, biting down on the moose's thick neck and twisted his head. A gratifying 'pop' sounded and the beast went limp.

Panting and nursing his shoulder, Mangarmyr leaned into the corpse. "I wish that could have been cleaner for you," he commented. "Forgive me."

Lifting his eyes, he saw the sun was moments from setting. Forcing himself to his feet, Mangarmyr tore into the dead moose. The hunger pains dwindled, but the fatigue remained. Especially after wrestling with the moose.

"All worn out?" a familiar voice chided.

Mangarmyr lifted his head. *Did I fall asleep?*

"It seems my plan worked, Brother."

Mangarmyr rose, steadying himself. It seemed Sharina was right. "Hatisven... So, you've finally come?"

The Fenrir curled his upper lip in a snarl. "I've always been here. Watching. Waiting. Biding my time."

"Where is Aruna?"

The Fenrir laughed. "Come find out…" He turned, the shadows molding themselves into a vortex. A blast of frigid wind burst through. "Follow if you dare, *brother*."

He vanished through the vortex, and Mangarmyr followed. When he emerged, Mangarmyr eyes fell on a vast sheet of white spread across a frozen landscape. Something felt wrong, though. The cold here was bitter, and the air full of malice. He shivered, which came as a shock. Yet Hatisven seemed unaffected.

"Welcome to Shundul. A land devoid of love and warmth."

Mangarmyr stiffened, eyes widening as he gazed at the misshapen snow-covered pines and evergreens. "A Fallen Realm…"

"No, Brother, a land created by one of the Vor Enshar. One of Father's first. Here, all her pain and emptiness manifest. Shundul sucks the warmth from your bones, leeching all emotion until you become a bitter, empty shell."

"So all this time…"

"She doesn't love you anymore, Skollander," he cut in. "You are just a painful memory to her. The cause of all her woes."

Mangarmyr lunged, jaws open. Hatisven jumped to his left side, avoiding his brother's jaws, and slammed his head into Mangarmyr's shoulder. Mangarmyr yelped, favoring his right side for support, and stumbled.

Hatisven laughed. "Not yet, Skollander. But soon, we will end this." The shadows hovering about him thickened and covered them both. "The demons here won't take kindly to us."

They stuck to the shadows and when 'night' fell on the frozen waste-land, the demons they passed paid them no mind in the open. Many were direct reflections of Shundul. Especially the giant humans made of ice. They were towering hulks, with pale aqua colored skin, white hair, and beards.

They talked about the realm like kings, and few challenged them. There were others, imps made of ice, and hulking brutes covered in thick fur. They had an ape-like appearance, but at their shoulders and knees sat a layer of ice. A pair of tusks, like a walrus, came down from their upper jaw.

Then there were the dark masses wandering about the snowy plains. They moved like sludge, but across its sickly surface, hundreds of faces appeared, then submerged themselves into the mass. They wailed as if in pain and the weaker demons that drew too close to them were enveloped, then devoured.

"The Broken," Hatisven commented. "Empty souls, drained of their essence and discarded. They are the trash of the realms. Wandering about as a collection of shattered memories from hundreds of mortals, each vying for dominance and identity."

"How horrific."

"You see now? How broken creation is? It's only a matter of time before it tears itself apart."

Mangarmyr felt the surrounding chill grow heavier. The pain in his heart deepening. He thought of Aruna, noting some of the emotion for her lacking in the depth. *I need to find her soon!*

"Where are you taking me?"

"To a very special place…"

They continued on, delving deeper into Shundul's depths. For a moment, Mangarmyr swore it felt as if they were passing between realms again, but the sensation was so subtle, he doubted his senses.

When they exited the passage, the world opened up, becoming a cavern so large the ceiling seemed impossibly out of reach. The chill cut deeper, and he shivered. Hatisven seemed pleased by his reaction, though still, the cold of this place didn't appear to bother the Fenrir.

"My den is near", he announced, plodding on.

Reluctant, Mangarmyr followed. More demons passed, still oblivious of them. The glow of the ice was dim enough, casting shadows the pair could cling to. It was unnerving. Though the Garou had a sense of how powerful he was, he knew that even one demon was more than enough for him to struggle against in his current state.

When they arrived at the den, two smaller Fenrir greeted them. Hatisven had released the shadowy shroud cloaking them and the smaller fallen spirts bowed their heads reverently.

"Welcome home," one said. Strangely, his fur was white.

"Leave us, go hunt or do as you will. But do not return without suitable prey." They lowered their gazes in acknowledgement, and bounded away, vanishing like ghosts. Hatisven continued on without a word, though his expectations were clear.

The cave itself was a labyrinth, twisting and turning with dozens of adjoining tunnels. Hatisven has chosen his battlefield well. No doubt he'd memorized the layout, granting him the advantage. When they reached the den, there she was, bound in icy chains.

Aruna looked haggard; bags lay under her eyes. She appeared too weak to stand and even in the cold her cheeks were right red and eyes bloodshot. Without thinking, Mangarmyr ran to her.

"My mate!" he cried. "Aruna, I'm here!" He nuzzled her with his muzzle, but she gave no response. Instead, his love stared at the cold rocky floor of the cave. "Aruna."

"She's been here too long," Hatisven explained matter-of-factly. "Her heart is dead inside. She will never help another or love you again. "I have killed the moon and none could stop me!"

Mangarmyr turned, frost wafting from his body. But even as he channeled his power, something felt off. The magic burned, cutting him deep within his essence. Hatisven seemed almost pleased with himself.

"Yes, Brother, give in. Purge your heart of all that warmth. Let bitterness fill you. Let Shundul take all you are!"

Mangarmyr stopped, glancing at Aruna from over his shoulder. He narrowed his eyes...something wasn't right. "You're not her...are you?"

"Are you blind? Who else would it be?" Hatisven asked.

He plodded closer, taking in her scent. The rot of a Fenrir was all over her. "What did you do?"

"What do you think?" he sneered, acting as if he had won some minor victory. "I mated with her. Over and over until she finally broke."

"But you said she hated me. Blamed me for all of this. Yet the female crumpled here can neither speak nor even acknowledge we're here."

"Broken toys, dear brother. Broken toys."

Surprisingly, Hatisven's response held no sting. Maybe Shundul was having its way after all. Mangarmyr searched his heart, yet the warmth he felt when he looked at her hadn't diminished. Then, he understood. *Part of me wanted to believe you. I wanted the pain to end. Somewhere deep down, I thought that would be easier.*

"Tell me, brother, how did you capture her?" Hatisven narrowed his eyes. "Are you really that powerful?"

A deep growl escaped the Fenrir's throat. "You doubt my power?" Hatisven shifted, growing to full size. Each of his heads focused their attention on Mangarmyr, their eyes radiating with malice.

Mangarmyr took a breath. "No, you are powerful. I've seen as much. But I also have seen your weakness. You fear Aruna's light, it hurts you. So, how did you capture her?"

Taking a deep breath, Mangarmyr turned, covering Aruna in a cloud of frost as he exhaled. A painful canine yelp followed and where Aruna once sat was a female Fenrir, partially shifted into a human-like form.

"You were only half lying." In his heart, Mangarmyr couldn't help but pity the poor fallen spirit. He had heard that such a thing was common among Fenrir. Yet seeing it brought him to anger. "I will set you free."

"Touch her and die! That is mine!"

Mangarmyr turned, his heart aching. The cold didn't seem as bad anymore. "There really is nothing left, is there?"

Hatisven stepped closer, a shadowy miasma gathering around his paws. "You... you actually thought to save me?"

"I had hoped, but I can say that is one thing Shundul has taken from me. I see things clearly now. The brother I had is gone."

Digging deep, muddling through the pain, Mangarmyr could feel Shundul try to retaliate as he drew on his power. It was like walking on sharp stones cutting into the pads of your feet. As he continued pushing through, Hatisven seemed to shrink, until they were eye level.

The Fenrir stared in disbelief, and for a moment, Mangarmyr sensed a hint of fear. "I was the stronger of us, brother."

"Not anymore!" Hatisven snapped. "I'm done with the game. You will be part of me for eternity. Here, there is no Cycle to return to. I would either turn you, or consume all of you."

"Then let's end this..."

They lunged at one another, jaws open wide. Mangarmyr tried avoiding Hatisven's other heads, but one managed to sink its fang into his shoulder. Yet as it did, the head closest to his bother's left shoulder left itself open enough to bite into its throat.

I satisfying yelp followed and the other head released. Without even concentrating, shards of ice formed around Mangarmyr and he flung them like knives at his brother. Hatisven conjured a cloak of shadows, devouring the icy shards, then at the same moment, summoned another to throw them right back at Mangarmyr.

On reflex, Mangarmyr took control of the snow at his fee. Forming an icy shield as the shards embedded themselves or bounced harmlessly off it. Hatisven's wounded head coughed up blood, but was still strong enough to be a threat.

The dance continued. Despite his wounds, Mangarmyr saw he still stronger. Hatisven, however, was still just as skilled with magic. Something he was definitely using to his advantage.

His brother put him on the defensive. There was plenty of shadow for him to manipulate, whereas the ice and snow were quickly becoming spend the more magic Mangarmyr poured his own power into it. Part of him longed to have an affinity with the earth and stone, but he wasn't that kind of spirit, even as Eldest. Though there were other Garou who had been Eldest, each had powers that differed with the elements.

Frantic, Mangarmyr took stock of his surroundings. Some of the cave supports were made of pure ice, though something was wrong with how they felt. Trying to keep from diverting his attention, he prodded deeper, horrified to learn that living essence made up the entire lattice of the massive shard's crystalline structure.

He sensed so much pain that it stole his focus, giving his brother an opening as the cloudy miasma cloaking Hatisven, surged around the icy shields he was controlling, and enveloped Mangarmyr. They became heavy, like the bonds shackling the broken Fenrir female to the stone wall.

Hatisven slung Mangarmyr to the floor of the den, his head smashing against its rough shod surface. The Fenrir wheezed as he approached, panting heavily to catch his breath. His wounded head seemed weak, as gasped for for air.

"It's over brother."

The miasma's touch burned. Mangarmyr felt his strength failing. He lifted his eyes toward Hatisven, then toward the broken Fenrir chained to the wall. She gazed back, her expression wrought with pleas for mercy. The cry of the crystalline pillar sang within Mangarmyr's spirit. It too begged for release, for an end to its suffering.

Then help me, he thought to it. *Help me and I will set you free...*

As if responding, the icy pillar cracked, causign the den to shudder violently. Hatisven paused, his focus momentarily weakened. Mangarmyr seized the moment, creating a hailstorm out of that ice and snow remained.

The flurry battered his brother, cutting and bludgeoning him. On reflex to shield himself, Hatisven let go, creating a bubble out of the miasma to deflect the brunt of the maelstrom. Mangarmyr stood, worn down, but not deterred. The pain from channeling his power in the dark realm was growing more than he could bear. His body was already growing numb and the icy touch of Shundul's influence pricked him once again.

I have to get out of here...

He prodded whatever the creature sealed inside the pillar was. It responded, cracking the support further. Other supports, feeling the strain, also began breaking. Tiny shard flew from them as fissures took shape across their surfaces. Mangarmyr reached to these broken shards, calling them to him and fashioning them into large knives.

Hatisven roared, thickening the bubble until the snowstorm the miasma absorbed the debris, dissolving it. He cut from head to paw, his right head hung limply while the other seemed just barely clinging to life. He limped closer, lips curled into a feral snarl.

"Nothing left, brother. You've exhausted all the ice in the room." A cloud formed above him, dividing itself into hundreds of tiny needled. As if to accent the end was nigh, he lengthened each needle. "Anything else to say?"

"Goodbye, brother."

Hatisven laughed, shifting his weight in a gesture to order the shadowy needles forward. Mangarmyr simple hung his head, causing the icy daggers hovering high above his brother to plummet, piercing his back and sides.

Hatisven's jaw fell slack and as he fell, the needles exploded randomly in every direction. Some even piercing him. Hit the stone floor, releasing his power, and shrinking in size. The needles became like giant spears, pelting the area around him. One even landed a hair's breadth from his nose.

"Clever," Hatisven gasped, his eyes barely open.

Mangarmyr rose, limped toward the fallen Fenrir. "I'm sorry," he said.

"Spare me your pity and end this."

Mangarmyr breathed deeply, covering his brother in a cloud of frost. Hatisven wailed as it began purifying his essence, but to Mangarmyr's horror, his form changed. The black sooty coast his brother once had was now ghost white.

His crimson eyes turned black, and in them, the Garou saw nothing but emptiness. While his wounds remained, Mangarmyr felt a change occur within the Fenrir. Something had been stripped away.

As he lay dying, Hatisven laughed. "I finally have it, yet I'm going to die. How poetic..." and with that, Hatisven breathed this last, dissipating into an icy mist.

Mangarmyr turned to the female Fenrir, then to the pillars. Risking more pain, he shifted into his human form. The process was excruciating. He approached the Fenrir, breaking her shackles. She fell limply to the stone floor.

"We get out of here together." She nodded, too weak to fight.

At the entrance to the main chamber, he paused, eyeing each icy pillar. Exhaling a frosty mist, it filled the chamber with loud shrieks resonating everywhere. One by one, the pillars collapsed, shattering like glass.

Mangarmyr saw something moving within the mist as the main chamber of the den became buried rubble. Moment later all was silent, and he hoped whatever it was trapped the ice had found peace.

The female Fenrir lifted her head. "If you still love her, focus on that. Fill yourself with it and Shundul will expel you. It hates that sickly emotion. It's the antithesis of its existence."

"How do you know this?"

"Hatisven would rant on and on about you. Even when…" she paused. "He was obsessed, spouting every thought whenever we were alone. He assumed you would lose the very thing you needed to escape."

Heeding her words, Mangarmyr focused his hear on Aruna. His moon. Like wildfire, his love for her ignited, and like a wounded animal, he sensed Shundul recoiling in disgust. The ice and stone quivered and cracked, as if enraged and a bitter cold washed over both him and the Fenrir.

A storm followed and amid the jagged rock and ice, just as quickly as it came, the storm subsided, and they were standing in the middle of an evergreen forest. Setting the female down, he reached out with his magic. It felt right. There was no pain. He turned back to her, but she was gone.

"Another time," he said. Seconds later, a wave of exhaustion slammed into him and Mangarmyr collapsed onto the forest floor.

***

The smell of burning pine and evergreen roused him alongside the aroma of freshly cooked meat. Mangarmyr lifted his head, seeing that he was once again a wolf. At the fire sat a woman and his heart leapt.

"Aruna..." he whispered.

She turned, eyes red. "I'm so sorry," she said.

He moved to stand, but she quickly stopped him. "Rest." He lay on his side, allowing her to cradle his large head in her arms. "There was so much I wanted to do. So much I should have done..."

She wouldn't stop crying, and he let her. Now wasn't the time for words. Gently he shifted his head into her and she cradled it ever so tightly.

"Forgive me?"

"Always," he replied.

"So you know?"

"As soon as I realized you weren't captured. That it was impossible for him to be strong enough, I understood."

"She made me stay away. I had to, for so many reasons."

"Aruna. It is okay. I am here now. Here with my precious moon."

She leaned over, kissing his muzzle. "I didn't know if it would be you or him. I prayed you would win. That he would lose, but it had to happen."

"I know, more than anyone I understand, now. Had he been allowed to roam freely, Hatisven would have become even more of a monster. Maybe even strong enough to harm you."

She nodded, then turned to the fire. Lifting his eyes, Mangarmyr saw that the food was ready.

Maybe I can finally have peace.

– Asger –

"That's it?"

Brandt shook his head. "No." He stood, moving to the window and opening the shutter. "Come here boy."

Asger came up behind him, his gaze following his uncle's at the night sky. It was still just as clear as when they first stepped into the house. The stars and Eske shone brightly.

"Look there, at that collection of stars. What do they look like to you?"

Asger followed his uncle's finger, noting the shape of where it trailed. "That's a wolf!"

Brandt smiled. "Indeed it is. Nothing how Eske crosses its path?"

Asger frowned. "Not you're making things up."

"Am I?" his uncle laughed. "This from the boy who moments ago was knee deep in his third mug of mead and sitting on the edge of his seat at my story."

Asger gave him a sour look. "Shut up."

Brandt laughed again. "Are you gonna pout or should I finish?" Asger took his seat at the table and his uncle followed. "Sharina knew that there was only one way to maintain the balance. Killing Mangarmyr, meant Aruna hating her and risking more strife. Keeping them separate would likely do the same for Mangarmyr and risk making the same thing that happened with Hatisven, happen to him."

"So, she gave a place in the heavens, but at a price. You see, one of the reasons Aruna had been away for so long was because she was pregnant."

Asger's mouth fell open.

"Aye, boy. She had to stay away to protect their children, the first dire wolves. Though those wolves differed from the ones we work with today. They were smarter and could speak. Part them was still spirit and they had power."

"So what happened? Why are they different?" Asger asked.

"The more they mingled with mortals, particularly the animals of their kind in the mortals realm, the less of their spirit nature passed on. These wolves were also mortal. Sharina had seen to that. Letting them roam free as immortal spirits was also a threat to the balance."

"That seems a bit cruel..."

"Is the life we live cruel and unfair?" his uncle asked. "We know the dangers and the risks of Sokoran life. Our actions breed consequence. If we work against ourselves, doesn't everyone suffer?"

Asger grew quiet. His uncle's words rang with a bit of truth. Sokoras didn't tolerate weakness. Selfish mistakes in this cold land cost lives. "Still... To have a family and be apart from it."

"Yet, look at the pens. I say his offspring have done quite well for themselves."

"So, they get to be together in the heaven then?"

"They do, but your Gran often mentioned. Mangarmyr is impatient. He chases the sun by day, to hasten the night. That way he can wait for his love in the night and lay with her when they cross paths."

"So she thought the months when the sun sets faster," Asger commented.

"Was when Mangarmyr was the most impatient. But he for eternity he will chase his moon, because he loves her."

"So it's a happy ending? Asger asked. "What of the darkness? You made it sound like there was something coming? Or did they prevent it?"

His uncle's expression changed. "The consequence..." he mused trailing off. "You know how the frost giants speak The Beast?"

Asger nodded. "They talk their father and mother often in their war cries. They speak of the Beast in their hunts."

"Kendezzar," he said, almost bitterly. "Do you know what he looks like?"

Asger shook his head.

"You should, I've already given you a description."

Asger stared at his uncle. "Hatisven?!"

Brandt nodded. "You see when Mangarmyr purified him, it didn't go like should have. Whatever shred of warmth or familial connection he once shared, was stripped from him. His essence was purified, but not in the way Mangarmyr intended."

"The fallen realms take and by attempting to purify Hatisven, he cut him off from The Cycle and bound him to Shundul."

"So the reason why the giants hate our wolves so much…"

"Is because of Kendezzar's hate for Mangarmyr and Aruna. He wants to eradicate every last dire wolf and take them as trophy's to flaunt before his brother and Aruna."

"Such a sad existence."

"I couldn't agree more." Brandt rubbed his eyes, noting how low the fire was getting.

"I think you're more tire than me, Uncle."

"I'm old," he chuckled. "I have an excuse. You best be heading home."

Asger nodded. "Da is probably laying on the floor passed out." His uncle's expression turned grim. "Ever since your mother dissapeared…"

"I know, Uncle," Asger replied bitterly. "But it couldn't be helped. I wish I could remember her."

"She was amazing and like you the wolves loved her."

"Good night, Uncle."

"Good night, Nephew."

Through the snow and icy air, Asger took a path through the houses that would lead him pack to the pens. Almost immediately the dire wolves there stopped, their eyes on him. It was eerie, but nothing new. Though tonight, something felt different.

The warrior looked up at the sky, his heart skipping in surprise at what he saw. There was an outline behind Eske. It was faint, yet soft enough to make out.

His thoughts turned inward. A sense of inspiration overtaking him. Brandt has always teased him about his poetry, yet in the moment, it seemed to right as the words came to mind:

"Oh beautiful moon shining bright

Oh beautiful moon guiding me through the night

The days were long and endless, the nights cold and bleak

But in the dark, an end to my lonliness did I seek.

I didn't know what you were when I first saw your light

I didn't know its warmth could fill me with such delight

Yet shining orb, hanging in my dark sky

Your beauty chased all away, bringing a tender tear to my eye.

So beautiful moon shining so bright

Beautfiul moon, who offered me her light.

Guide me evermore until the end

From this night on and eternal, for from the heavens did you decend."

SNOWBOUND

The bitter cold burned his lungs, stabbing at them like tiny knives. His breath came out in thick clouds of fog as he panted, fighting for breath. *How did it come to this?*

Finn wanted to laugh at himself for asking, but it was human nature to ask the most ridiculous things at the worst times. The frosty air bit through his yak hide gloves and boots, cutting into his fingers and toes, numbing them as he frantically trudged through the snow, fleeing his pursuers. But it wasn't just the cold tearing into him or Norenheim's murderous icy wind harassing him. The deep gash from the giant's lash on his leg did well to add to his woes.

He cringed at the winds whipping around him, bundling his arms around him, and daring to cast a glance at the pines and evergreens at his back. His enemy was out there somewhere and eager for the hunt. It was just another in a long list of rituals the Norens practiced.

So much of their belief revolved around their ancient traditions. Around a being they sometimes referred to as 'All-Father'. Kennings were one such example. A telling of tales citing one's deeds. Sometimes it was metaphor, other times it was embellishment. But it was of the few traditions of the Norens that bled into Sokoran life.

Finn clenched his fist. Fingers stinging from the cold. *I almost envy you*, he thought, glancing behind him at the forest.

To a frost giant, the cold was like a warm summer day, the wind a temperate breeze and the snowflakes an afternoon shower. Here in the north, the advantage belonged to his enemy. Only the border offered salvation, though even that might not deter the brute.

Finn thought of home, of his blessed Sokoras. Perhaps an Immortal was watching and would grant him favor. Perchance he might happen across one of his brothers, a fellow Ranger. Perhaps.

Staring at the night sky, the moon's soft glow lit up the clouds, and where they broke, the stars peered through. Eske shone brightly and somewhere lurking behind him sat Aruna. The Twins, as some called them. Legends speak of Aruna helping those in need and though he wasn't much for superstition. Finn half hoped the stories were true.

The skies were clearer in Norenheim, unlike Sokoras, which was under constant cloud cover most of the time. The reason for this was simple enough. Norenheim wasn't a cursed land. At least most Sokorans believed their homeland cursed.

There was a legend from ancient times. One that spoke of black clad invaders scouring the land. Supposedly, the frost giants fought with them. After winning the war against their enemies, out of spite, they wove a vile curse over the country. Though they deceived the frost giants, keeping them in the dark about their actions.

It was because of their dark magic of the invaders that Sokorans burned the dead on a pyre instead of burying them. Finn thought of the last great pyre, of how many frost giants they had burned after one patrol he'd been on. Part of him regretted treating their dead so disrespectfully. He and his brothers had dug a pit, setting the bodies ablaze. Though they had been the aggressors, crossing the border on yet another raid, they fought well. But it had to be done. If it wasn't, and the person held regrets in life, their corpse would rise to feed on the flesh of the living.

A draconic roar tore Finn from his thoughts. It was distant, possibly still miles away. But carried well on the wind. *Scriving frost giants and their dragons.*

Leaning against a nearby pine, Finn took a moment to catch his breath, scanning the clouds, hoping for a break that would reveal The Weeping Maiden in the heavens. She was up there somewhere, one of many constellations, and if found, the Western Star would be close by and be his guide home. The Western Star had another name, Skollander's Eye. It was part of another constellation, one that sat perfectly in the moon's path.

Squinting, Finn glimpsed her through a slight break in the clouds, and his heart leapt. After a few moments, he found Skollander's Eye, and he pressed on, his thoughts turning to his wife, Saer. He pictured her soft blue eyes and long, braided hair. Just imagining the warmth of her embrace was enough to stave off the bitter chill in the air.

I'll be home soon, dearest.

Another roar reached his ears, as if to discourage him, and drew Finn back to the present. It was closer this time, pressing the sense of urgency and the need to escape his pursuer. He scanned the surrounding pines. They sat packed together just enough to keep him hidden from the air, but a dragon's sense of smell was especially keen. He touched the bandage on his leg and grimaced at the bloodstains from his wound. It needed to be cleaned, changed, and the bandages burnt. Still, one whiff of burning pine and the dragon would be on top of him in a moment.

Lady, have mercy, he prayed. *Grant me a refuge for the night.*

The druids of Yggsid often spoke of the Lady. That she was ever watchful over her faithful and protective of those who respected The Cycle. Finn never gave her or the other Immortals much thought. Random coincidence seemed the most reasonable conclusion, but a druid once asked him, 'How much coincidence needs to happen before you find the truth?'.

Trudging on, exhaustion gnawed at him. *How many miles have I gone?*

Stumbling, Finn caught himself against another pine, his eyes glimpsing a break in the dense snow against the pale moonlight. He lifted his head to the sky, blinking for a moment. Finn thought he saw the sliver of a second moon behind Eske. He shook his head and pushed forward.

Skulking closer to the break, he dug some of the powder away and his premise on faith shook. The opening was a small hole, just large enough for a man to fit through. His heart leapt, scarcely believing what he was looking at.

A snow fox den? Finn eyed the opening. It was unusually large, but nonetheless, a hopeful answer to his prayers.

Crawling inside, wincing from the pain in his leg, Fin slid down the shaft, reaching the bottom. Once inside, the soft echo when he hit the floor hinted that the chamber was larger than one might think. His eyes watered at the slight warmth within the chamber. It wasn't much, but at least it was a shield from the bitter wind outside.

Moonlight crept its way down the shaft. Though dim, Eske's elegant rays cast enough light to leave him frozen in place upon revealing the skeletal remains near the opening. Straining his eyes, Finn reached to touch the bones. To his surprise, his fingers brushed against several sets, some small, probably whatever the fox had hunted. But when they drifted across a much larger bone, he blinked. No fox could have been strong enough to drag one of this size into the chamber.

Following the shape of the bone, Finn's fingers came across a frozen, rotting hand much larger than his own. In its grip was a skeggox and by comparison to his stature, the large axe would have to be wielded two-handed to be of any use. For a frost giant, however, holding such a weapon in one hand would be a simple matter.

Feeling around further, Finn came across tatters of cloth and bits of chainmail around the severed arm. Taking a small femur he found, Finn wrapped some of the cloth around it and took out a pair of spark stones from his belt pouch, lighting the cloth. The added warmth was a blessing. The light of the flames gave a clearer view of the den. With the darkness forced back, it was certain the severed arm had indeed belonged to a frost giant. Judging by what remained, and the state of decay of the hand, the arm had been here for several months.

The firelight also revealed the chamber's size. Fin realized he could almost stand to his full height. No snow fox could have dug this, and the number of bones was too numerous. Some of the animal remains were too big for a fox to have taken on. Waving the small torch around,

Finn reflexively gasped at the remains of a snow leopard across the chamber. It was frozen, and mostly bone.

That makes more sense now. Snow leopards are as much opportunists as they are predators. They'll take out a snow fox in their dens and widen the space for themselves.

Finn quickly checked for side chambers. If this was the larder, then the leopards would have a place dug out to sleep and another for a back exit. Sure enough, two more chambers connected to the larder, both empty, but one had a wider opening angling up to the outside.

He glanced back at the skeletal limb, then at the leopard's remains. "You must have found some poor sod's corpse in the snow and took what you could for yourself. Too bad for you, few creatures can stomach a frost giant's flesh."

Another roar rang out, and he froze. Though muffled slightly, he could tell it came from just above. Fin quickly doused the light and curled up for warmth. A second draconic roar sounded and fear overtook his heart. The sound of felled pine trees, followed by the loud thud of the dragon's heavy body landing on the ground, came next.

They're just above me! Heavy footfalls followed. The rider had dismounted. He spoke in the thick guttural tones of giantspeech, and a slight hiss came after as if the dragon were responding to him. The giant was talking with his dragon. A deeper, rasping voice responded, its speech laced with serpentine tones.

The giant spoke again. This time, his tone was harsher than before. There was another hiss, as if in disagreement, and the giant raised his voice. It sounded like he was threatening the beast. Finn held his breath in the den's silence. Minutes later, an ear-piercing shriek rang out, followed by the sound of more trees being felled and sooner after, all was still.

Finn lay frozen in terror's grip, his heart thrumming loudly. Somehow, he found the courage to gather himself up and light what little scraps of cloth remained. As he crept toward the back entrance of the den, worry set in. Through the dim torchlight, he spied what appeared to be a branch blocking the shaft leading outside. At first glance, from the angle of the shaft, it appeared still attached to the pine tree it had come from, blocking the exit.

As he tugged on the branch, to Finn's relief, it came loose, and he drug it into the larder. He then placed his small torch down, though it was more like a tiny candle now, and taking the dead giant's axe, Finn began chopping the branch into smaller sections.

With each swing, his arms felt like lead, the fatigue of running from the giant, and his dragon had hit full force. Finn pushed through it, knowing the branch would be his salvation. It represented the warmth his body desperately needed. Thankfully, the axe was still sharp, its weight making the effort easy.

Upon finishing, his eyes grew heavy, and the pangs of hunger stabbed at his gut. His leg burned, and upon checking the wound in the dying light, it didn't look good. There was an angry red tinge around the gash left in the wake of the giant's lash. Because of the cold, some of the blood had frozen and would need to be cleaned from the wound.

I can't let you get infected. The thought of searing the wound made him cringe, but there weren't any herbs on hand to treat it properly. Not unless he was extremely lucky, and some were growing at the base of the pines outside. Fin sighed and leaned back against the dirt wall of the den. His eyes fell to the shadows cast by the dying firelight and the bundle of pine in front of him.

"Giving up already, my love?"

Finn's heart skipped a beat, his mind screaming that the voice he'd heard was impossible. He turned my head, seeing a lithe figure in the shadows just inside the den's secondary chamber. The figure moved into the dimming light and he blinked, trying to convince himself that his eyes had deceived him.

"Saer?" His beloved smiled, her golden hair cast into a single braid that fell down her chest. Her long-sleeved dress was the same heavy gray linen tones, with the blue aproned pullover she wore often.

She smiled wider, coming closer. "Of course, my Heart of Hearts. Who else would I be?"

"Saer, I fought and fought until I finally broke free. After the battle, I woke up and saw they had captured me. They threatened to feed me to their dragons so many times."

Finn felt ashamed, knowing he must sound like a whimpering child. His eyes watered, expecting a disapproving look from his wife, but instead, he only saw warmth and compassion on her face.

"Shh," she said, kneeling and taking him into her arms. "It's okay, Finn. But you must not give up. You must be strong." Tears trickled down Finn's cheeks as he held her. The warmth of her body and the gentle caress of her lips as she kissed his bearded cheek ignited his spirit and filled his soul. "I know, Finn. I know. But you must wake up. I'm waiting."

I paused and stared into her soft blue eyes. "Wake up?"

She nodded, her face growing stern. "Wake up, my Heart of Hearts. Wake up now!"

Finn's eyes fluttered open, his hands numb and feet stinging. It was only a dream, but also an ill omen. "Death terror," he whispered. In Sokoras, such dreams and hallucinations meant you were close to death, that the Keeper's Shadow hung over you.

Frantically, he gathered up the pine wood, fumbling with it as he piled it near the larder's exit shaft. *Please let there be enough of a draft to carry the smoke outside.*

In the off chance the dragon and its master were still lurking about, the smoke from the burning pine might give him away. Either way, Finn knew he would die, but better later than sooner.

Taking a piece of the branch he'd chopped up, Finn slid it across the skeggox's sharp edge. His fingers stung as he gripped the small log, almost making it impossible to hold on to. When finished, he took another piece of wood, split it and took the shavings he'd made, placing them on the split piece's flattened side.

It only took a few breaths after igniting it with the spark stones for the embers to grow into a decent flame. Carefully nursing it, Fin fed smaller bits of the branch to the growing fire until it could stand on its own. As the flames grew, warmth spread through the larder.

He knew it should have taken longer. Pine was like a sponge with water, but still he welcomed the ease at which the sparks bit into the kindling. To Finn, the fire was like the first rays of dawn; the heat covering him like a shadow. With each breath, it filled his lungs, warming his chest, and he removed his gloves, noting the pale tones of his fingertips.

As he settled in, understanding flashed in his mind. He was alive and had survived. The joy and sorrow of the moment overtook him, and Finn wept. Though he knew it was fleeting, the fact he still lived became a comfort words couldn't express.

His joy came from the knowledge that despite everything, he had endured everything the frost giants threw at him. But his sorrow was for those who weren't so fortunate. For his brothers, who the giants had grown tired of and dealt with as they saw fit. For the captives they had taken and hadn't survived Norenhiem's harsh conditions and the ones who they had fed to their dragons.

He eyed the skeggox across his lap. His heart screamed for revenge as he gripped its haft. Despite his rage, Finn shook his head at such a foolish notion. "What could one ranger with an axe do against so many?"

Reluctantly, he quelled his rage as best he could, letting the crackling of the fire and the smell of burning pine distract him. With the distraction, hunger tore into him, giving him focus.

I need to find food.

Luckily, pine trees had edible parts. The cones, the needles, and even the deeper layers of bark were just some things one could use for survival. The sap was also useful for treating wounds and fighting infection.

With his body warmed, and the feeling returning to his feet and hands, Finn took stock of the bones around him. His eyes fell on the snow leopard's remains and its femur. Taking in hand, he tested its strength and began cutting away at one end, shaping it into a point. As daggers went, it was useful and capable.

"You may not cut," Finn mused. "But at least I can use you to pick away the bark on the pine trees outside."

Weakly, after stoking the fire, Finn exited the larder and crept up to the larger shaft in the next chamber. He cautiously poked his head near the edge of the opening, eyeing the branches clogging it up. He tugged at them. Some came loose, while others clung limply to the trunk of the pine they belonged to.

After working them all free, Finn piled them up, his eyes once again growing heavy. "I'm wasting energy," he mumbled.

With the shaft cleared, he began his ascent, using the shiv he fashioned from the leopard's femur as an anchor while dragging the large skeggox behind him. It only took a couple minutes to reach the exit, but the biting wind hit him full force once he pulled himself out of the den.

Finn gazed at the smattering of trees the dragon had felled when it landed. He shuddered, imagining the beast's size. Most of the dragons serving the frost giants were young, but this one must have been older. The area looked like some sort of terrible storm had hit. Trees lay everywhere in the packed snow, creating a small clearing.

"It's no wonder you missed me," he commented. Again, his premise on faith was shaken. The trees had fallen just right to keep the den hidden from the giant. Their argument must have been over what the dragon smelled versus what the giant saw. "Let's hope you assumed I was flattened by the debris."

With so many trees to forage from, hunger wouldn't be a problem. He quickly set about gathering pinecones, bark and, if there was enough, any sap he could bleed out of the fallen trees. Normally it would be too cold, but if there was enough to be heated, that would at least be something.

"It seems the Lady smiles upon me again," he mused.

It took several trips to harvest enough and by his fourth, Finn had grown ever more sluggish and on the verge of passing out. As he made his way to the den, over the wind gusts, he heard a low guttural rumbling. His heart sank as he turned slightly to his left and he dropped the last bundle of provisions he'd gathered.

A grizzlar with the whitest of coats was staring at him. The beast was enormous, its body burly and strong. A low rumbling groan escaped the grizzlar's throat as it sniffed the air. It stood to its full height, balancing itself on its hind legs in a show of strength.

Finn gripped the skeggox, fighting off his exhaustion. *Calm,* he told himself. *If I let fear rule me, it will see me as prey.* The grizzlar dropped to all fours and roared. Finn froze. *Scriving yak scrag!*

The beast charged, its heavy breaths sounding like thunder as it closed the gap between them. Finn braced himself, uncertain if he'd make it into the den in time. The opening was only a few feet away. He widened his stance, knowing the next few moments would be crucial.

The beast lumbered ever closer, like a yak on a rampage. Finn steadied his breathing, quelling his fear, with the giant's axe at the ready. He would only get one strike and should he fail, the great bear would find him a satisfying meal. *Lady, guide my axe.*

The grizzlar rose to tackle Finn, attempting to use its enormous body to crush him under its weight. Finn's eyes drooped, but he recovered in time and pivoted, whirling the skeggox around in a wide arc.

The axe's sharp edge glided across the grizzlar's throat and Finn fell back, landing on the ground just a hair out of its reach. A gurgling moan followed, and the ranger watched the grizzlar bleed out as it lay in the bloody snow, struggling for breath and choking on its own blood.

Finn winced, regretful that it hadn't died instantly. "I promise not to let your death go to waste," he whispered reverently. Finn raised his axe and severed the bear's head from its shoulders, ending its suffering. "If the Keeper has a place for you, I hope it's a paradise."

Gazing at its body, Finn knew he had his work cut out for him. Hunger pangs sliced at his gut. "I have to eat first and regain some strength."

Taking the Skeggox, he shoved it down the entrance to the den and slid down the shaft. The warmth greeting him inside was a blessing, thawing him out and chasing away the winter chill. Once in the larder, he fed the fire, keeping it up and cleaning the pine nuts from the pinecones he'd gathered. He ate the bark too, but also heated some of it to boil the sap out and apply it to his leg wound.

Whatever he couldn't salvage, Finn burned. Keeping the fire alive was too important. He took a moment to rest, fighting off sleep. The bear needed to be cleaned, not only for food and its fur, but also to keep scavengers from ruining the carcass.

Finn propped the skeggox up, leaning into it as if his life depended on it, while searching for the strength to stand. He focused his thoughts on home and his wife. Of her smile and warm embrace. He pulled himself to his feet, his gaze cast toward the adjoining chamber.

"I can rest when I'm dead."

***

The smell of roasted bear meat on the fire clawed at some deep, forgotten primal instinct. It tempted Finn to tear a chunk of it prematurely from the makeshift spit he'd fashioned. Patience, however, won out, and he resisted. What meat he couldn't immediately prepare had to be buried in the snow to keep it cool and fresh. It was a common trick ravens often used to stash any food they scavenged.

The grizzlar's pelt lay stretched tightly between two long pine branches. Finn had cut notches into them, and pinned thin sticks into the holes he'd made to keep the pelt taught as it dried. Preparing the beast's hide had become a task of its own. There were so few resources outside of his own urine and the bear's innards to make a pelt of decent quality. But having it was better than freezing to death outside as he made the long trek home.

Turning the bear's skull into a bowl made part of the process easier. The snow outside could be melted, boiled, and turned into potable water alongside tree bark to make a tannin. While the process was cruder than what a real tanner would do, again, it was still better than nothing. The skull also made turning the pine sap into an antiseptic more helpful in tending to the gash on his leg.

Once sharpened, the beast's claws became excellent knives, which made for cleaning its carcass easier than using the skeggox or the bony shiv he'd made. Finn eyed the roasting meat, noting its color and taking a claw, he cut strips of it off the spit. As the meat hit his tongue, his senses melted from the flavor. Though unseasoned, it carried a texture similar to deer, but mildly sweeter.

When he leaned back against the den wall and with solid food in his stomach, Finn felt himself slowly drifting off. His body begged for rest after spending so much time cleaning the grizzlar's carcass. It simply had nothing left to give.

"Still so much to do," he mumbled as he passed out.

"*Finn...*" came a soft, ethereal whisper. "*Finn... wake up, my love. Time is short!*"

Finn's eyes fluttered open. The fire was almost out. His body ached and the heavy dregs of sleep weighed him down. *Am I dying?* Even in the den's warmth, he felt a chill. Something was off, though he couldn't place what it was.

A howled echoed in the night, filtering down the shaft where the fire lay. Weakly, Finn gazed up the shaft, past the wisps of smoke and flame. The night sky showed the subtle hints of dawn, with a line of light softly cutting across the treetops.

Pulling himself up, he threw a few more logs on the fire. Cutting a few strips of meat from what was left on the spit, Finn turned his attention to the pelt. "A few more hours," he muttered. "Definitely not the prettiest thing I've prepared, but thankfully your insides, bear, helped in saving it."

He checked his leg, taking some of the sap he'd preserved from the felled trees and reapplied it to his wound. The red coloring around the edge had softened. He took strips of pelt he'd cut and set them against the wound, bandaging it as best he could.

Over the next few hours, Finn gathering up the provisions for his journey. Using the skeggox, he chopped up more branches and fashioned them into a type of 'sled'. To keep it together, he cut grooves in the wood so they would 'snap' in place like a puzzle, then using the strips of the soft flesh of an evergreen tree he'd found, he lashed them together and sealed with it a paste made from sap and charcoal.

With the last of the soft evergreen flesh, Finn wove the strips together into a cord, taking care not to make it too taut or the fibers would snap and be useless. Taking the charcoal paste, he lathered it over the cords to increase their tensile strength and set them near the fire. With the sled finished and the paste needing time to dry, Finn took the meat he'd stored and cooked it, eating some of it while returning the rest to the snow, keeping it preserved.

As evening set in, he finished gathering the rest of his provisions and checked the grizzlar's pelt. It was nearly ready, a few more hours, a bit more tannin, some heat, and it would be finished. With all his preparations nearly complete, Finn turned his attention to his leg.

The color was better. The swelling had gone down, and while his leg still hurt, Finn found hope that infection hadn't set in. He cleaned the wound, using some of the water he'd boiled in the bear's skull, and covered it. A howl drew his attention up the shaft.

"Dire wolves," he muttered. "Let's hope you pass on." It wouldn't take much for the wolves to dig their way in from the den's entrance. Finn tossed a few bones on the fire and wood scraps. His thoughts drifted to home and to his wife.

How long have I been gone? He wondered. *A few weeks maybe?* As he thought back, trying to get his bearings on how much time had passed, Finn fell asleep. The fatigue of all his preparations setting in.

***

"Daydreaming again, Finn?" a familiar voice called. Finn blinked, casting a glance at his surroundings. "Finn, are you well?"

Finn glanced over his shoulder, his eyes widening at the sight of Arn's rugged face. His friend's brow was drawn together, his lips taut with concern. Then it all came back to him. They, along with two dozen other Rangers, were under contract to patrol the border.

Finn half smiled. "It's nothing, just a little homesick."

Arn grinned. "With a wife as beautiful as yours, I'd be homesick too," he winked. "I might 'accidentally' forget to take a contract or two. She's definitely worth a reprimand from Huntsman Eirik."

"Hey, don't be eyin' my wife. You've only got one good one left as it is."

Arn fell into a riotous laugh, nearly falling from his horse. "Then it's a blessing I can still notice her," he teased.

"Let's hope we all make it back home in one piece." Arn nodded, casting his gaze east, toward Norenheim. "You feel it too," Finn commented. "It's like the winds are whispering to us."

"Death," Arn muttered, touching his nonexistent left eye.

Silence fell between them, and Finn studied the other Rangers with them. They seemed just as uneasy. Everyone was mounted, a rare commodity in Sokoras. Horses were a premium and only used for contracts like this. To own a horse, said something about a person's standing in the north. Further south, in Henrik's domain, the old Thran trained the Rangers contracted to him on how to ride dire wolves. He was strict, though. No Ranger was permitted to share his secret for taming the beasts upon the penalty of death.

"I swear," Arn said, breaking the silence, "If I ever find that giant that took my eye, I'll make sure he loses both of his!"

Finn winced, remembering a skirmish with the Norens a year ago. One of the brutes backhanded Arn off his horse, nailing him around his left eye socket. The impact was so severe that ruptured his eye. Arn never got over it, and most days wore an eyepatch. But not today. It was like he hoped the same giant from a year ago would show himself and give the seasoned Ranger a chance for revenge.

"You mangled his calf with your axe, leaving him with a bad limp, if I remember."

Arn nodded, his expression hardening. "That I did, so if I ever see him again, I'll know. I'll make sure he sees the Keeper before he passes on."

An icy wind whipped up around their group at the mention of the Immortal. Finn didn't like the feel of it. Somehow, its touch was ominous. People often said that you could tell if the Keeper's shadow loomed over you. There were always signs.

"Finn, get your sword." Arn's tone sent the hairs on the back of Finn's neck standing straight. "My eye aches."

Finn cringed. Normally, when Arn made a comment like that, he was only partly joking. This time, however, he was deadly serious. Arn made a subtle hand motion to the other Rangers, and each reached for their weapons.

He scanned the pines, searching for a hint of something. Silence and wind greeted him, though Finn felt a heaviness in the air. "Bowmen, ready!" Arn commanded in a harsh whisper. Four rangers sheathed their swords and grabbed composite bows from the cradles on their saddles. They nocked arrows, eyes hawkish for any sign of movement among the pines.

"Let's hope that new poison from Yggsid pays off." Arn simply nodded, placing a finger to his lips. Finn bit his lip, regretting that he'd said anything at all.

Frost giants were incredibly resilient, though they had a low tolerance for heat. The poison gifted to them by the druids had no effect on humans, aside from a slight fever and nausea. For a frost giant, a fever could be deadly, especially if it has a rapid onset.

Another stiff wind blew through, stirring the top layer of snow around them. The clouds above blanketed the sky like a morbid shadow. Their tinge was darker than usual. Please don't let there be a storm brewing.

Minutes passed, and still no sign of any giants. Ard shifted his reins, turning his horse southward, when the blare of a horn stopped him. Moments later, a spear twice his size landed a few paces in front of him.

Ard's horse reared in shock and the big man clung to the saddle horn to keep from being thrown off. "Fall back!" he ordered. The rangers bolted to the west just as more spears rained down, some landing where the horses had stood only a moment ago.

Another horn blared in Finn's ears, and he glanced behind him. Between the gaps in the trees, two dozen giants came into view. A few still held spears, while the rest held a sword or skeggox alongside large, round shields.

"Archers!" Ard shouted.

The bowmen whipped around, aiming for the spearmen. The distance between them was great, but perchance they might clip them or pierce their chainmail enough for the poison to prick the skin. One cut would be all they needed.

The four of them loosed their arrows, focusing on the closest giant. He raised his shield, deflecting all but one arrow which pierced his left arm. The bowmen immediately fell back, catching up with their brothers.

"That's one," Ard panted. Another set of spears followed, but each ranger deftly maneuvered their horses in time to avoid being skewered. Ard reined his horse to a halt, the other rangers following suit. The spearmen drew their weapons, and as one, the frost giants began banging their weapons against their shields in a slow advance.

Finn saw Ard freeze, his right eyes narrowing and face hardening as he stared at the line of giants. "Forger's beard," he spat, his tone full of venom. "It's him!"

Finn traced where his old friend was staring, his eyes widening at the sight of one giant with a severe limp. The brute's leg was braced with some kind of metal harness around it. It seemed to help support his weight.

The dull thud of the giant's advance vanished in the moment, and Finn's heart sank. *No, Ard. Keep focused, we have to play this smart or we're dead!*

***

A sharp howl stirred Finn from his sleep with each breath he took, burning his lungs as he gasped for breath. The touch of the frigid air caressed his cheeks, and he looked toward the fire. Only a smoldering pile of ash remained of the small blaze he had worked so hard to keep lit.

Even the makeshift spit lay charred, brittle, and crumbling to the touch from his negligence. Judging by the bones he'd thrown in, several hours had passed and while not completely ashen, their usefulness as fuel was long past.

"Another dream," Finn muttered. He took the last of the bones from the larder, and piled them neatly together. He then added more pine from the fallen trees he had cut the day before and used his spark stones to light them. It took a moment, but the fire came back to life and its heat filled the den once more.

Finn gazed up the shaft beside the firepit. Dawn showed no signs of coming. He stared into the fire as it danced atop bone and pinewood. "I suppose it's time."

Gathering himself up, he checked the grizzlar's hide. Though it was rough in a few places, it would do. He set about cutting what he needed to make pouches and cords to tie them shut. Because of the bear's size, there was plenty of material to use.

Once he finished dressing the hide, Finn packed his provisions in the pouches he'd made. It was enough to last three or four days if he rationed it. The bear's meat would help with that, and whatever spoiled could be used in a fire.

Leaving everything by the den's entrance, he cast a glance back at the larder. A small part of him was reluctant to leave the safety the den offered behind. "I know I've never prayed to you properly before, Great Lady, but thank you for your kindness."

As if to show his sincerity, Finn took a fox skull, carefully bored two holes in the top of it and clipped the ends of two pine branches, placing them in the openings. Taking two more sticks, he crossed them, after placing both underneath the skull on the ground and tracing the outline of an axe head at their ends.

While it lacked the braided outlines and other adornment, it was as close of an approximation as Finn could muster. The Staghorn was a symbol of Yggsid and Huntsmen Eirik. The Huntsman's standard was darker in tone than the druid's version. He'd adopted it shortly after being appointed Huntsman over the Sokoran Rangers, citing it was in gratitude for a debt he owed the druids of Yggsid.

Kneeling before the totem, Finn quickly whispered another word of thanks to the Lady before focusing on moving his provisions outside and onto the sled. It was an arduous task, his leg protesting every time he pulled himself from the den's entrance. Yet he pressed on, biting through his discomfort.

Hours passed, and the sun reached its zenith. The cold bit where it could grab hold, but thanks to the bear's pelt, its grip wasn't nearly as potent as it would have been without it. The sled glided decently enough across the snow, though there were moments when its skids sunk too deep in and had to be dug out. Still, Finn found himself encouraged by his progress.

His leg was holding up. The swelling had lessened significantly, and the pigment was returning to normal. He stopped to clean the wound, making a fire, and melting the snow in the bear's skull. He also cleaned the hide bandages he'd made, heating them in the skull, then drying them out.

It was a good thing the sky was clear. It made it easier to track his direction. At night, the stars would be a better guide, ensuring he hadn't deviated too far north or south as he headed west. It was one of the first things you learned as a Sokoran Ranger. Tracking was the second. Most Sokorans learned to track from a young age, but Finding was a skill Rangers only taught to their own.

It came from the idea that all sentient beings share a sympathetic connection with objects personal to them. To the eye it looked like an ethereal thread and no matter the distance, so long as that person was alive, you could follow them anywhere. It only worked on one person at a time, and the longer the object remained out of the owner's possession, the weaker the thread was.

"Saer, I swear, when I get home, I'm going to ask for two clippings of your hair. Scriving giants, I had to leave it in my pack... If only Ard had listened!"

A draconic cry caught his ear. Finn threw himself to the ground, covering himself with the grizzlar's hide. *Please let it smell the bear and not me!*

The thrusting whoosh of air passed through overhead, the beast's wings booming louder than his beating heart. A shadow glided past, some of it blocked by the dense smattering of trees. The pine trees' shadows were long, and dusk was setting in. Rumor was, frost dragons had poor eyesight at this hour, meaning they depended heavily on their sense of smell.

"I know you're alive Ranger!" a thunderous voice cried out. "The bones told me so! To think you've stayed hidden for so long and survived my homeland is a feat worthy of a kenning! You have my respect. It will be my honor to hunt to and take your head to be a trophy in my hall."

I'd love you to kill you myself, giant, but I seek survival over vengeance.

"I will be sporting," the giant announced. "The border to Beirkonugr lies one hundred miles ahead of you. If you reach the border before I catch you, then I win the hunt and your life is forfeit. If you cross the border, then I will not pursue. But if you choose to fight me and survive at any time during the hunt, you will go free and earn my dragon as a reward."

It's a lie! Finn told himself. Giants had no honor. Everyone in Sokoras knew this. They're butchers and raiders.

The rush of air between the dragon's wings continued echoing overhead. The frost giant was circling. "Shall I take a Blood Oath? Will that give you proof of my words? Know that I could easily level the surrounding pines, hoping one might crush you. Frustvivla could easily make it so. She may not see you, but her nose tells her something is amiss."

Finn clutched the snow between his gloved fingers. *One hundred miles... At a fast pace, it would take me a day and a half. With my provisions, two days.*

"Call to me if you agree and we shall make the oath. Cower and I will level this area and pick it over for your corpse!"

Saer... His heart ached, longing for her. Finn knew he had no choice. *Great Lady of the Green, Of the Forests and the Land, let me make it home.*

Gathering his courage, Finn stood, the bear's pelt falling to his feet and into the snow. "I'm here, giant!"

A draconic roar echoed a few yards away and as the beast landed, it knocked aside the pines in its way. As Finn laid eyes on the dragon, his heart slid up his throat. The beast's size seemed inconceivable. It was nearly seventy feet or longer. For such an old dragon would be alive among the giants, meant that it was smarter and more clever than others of its kind.

When his enemy dismounted, Finn's eyes fell to the giant's left leg. It was encased in the same metal harness he'd seen before. The apparatus was shaped around it for support, though he walked with a limp. *You're the one who killed Ard!*

"I know that look," the frost giant said as a smile crossed his pale features. His beard and hair were white, his eyes deep blue. "You want to fight me, to avenge your brothers!" He laughed. "You and I aren't so different, Ranger. We may stand on different sides, but your people and mine have one goal. Survival."

"And raiding us each year accomplishes this?" Finn spat.

"Mother Numa birthed us, filled our hearts with the desire for conquest. All-Father Naesir commands we hunt, that the world is ours for the taking. Kendazzar taught us to track, to be the apex of all things. Is not survival woven into such things?"

"You plant crops where none should be. Fill storehouses with grain and foods we cannot. You exist as part of our cycle. Our prey that we should conquer and take. But we know we must have restraint. Take too much prey and the stores become empty. We would starve. So we honor Mother Numa, All-Father Naesir and The Beast, by finding a balance between these things."

"And if we were to teach you these things? Would the raids stop?"

The giant laughed. "Would you take the plow from the yak and till the ground yourselves? Would you fight the bear without an axe or bow? Perhaps you could tame the winds without magic... No Ranger, we would learn, but we would never stop. To do so is heresy and makes us unworthy of our All-Father, Mother and The Beast."

Finn curled his lip. "Make your oath, giant. It is nearly dark, and a hunt should begin at dawn!"

"I will make my oath when you make yours," the giant replied.

"An animal makes no oath. For prey simply does what it can to survive."

The giant cracked a smile, his eyes falling to the skeggox partially covered in bear hide. "Rightly said. It is good when your quarry knows its place." The giant drew his seax, taking the dagger across his palm. Blood flowed from the wound as he clenched his fist and spoke. "I swear on my life and honor that should you cross into Beirkonugr, I will not pursue. I swear that should I catch you and you offer to fight me, I will allow you to go free if you win. I swear only to take your life I defeat you in mortal combat or you submit and give up after being caught. I swear that once free, my dragon will take you home and she will belong to you forevermore."

He held out the knife, though in Finn's hands it was like a small shortblade. Fin cut his own hand, and they clasped them together. "I swear to abide by the rules you have stated and not betray your trust."

A warmth spread between their hands. The frost giant winced in discomfort, but said nothing. Finn felt a bond form between them, one that would bind their spirits together. It was like someone had placed a fishing hook inside his heart and drawn the line taut. Blood Oaths were common among allies and enemies alike. It was a way to establish trust between two parties. Should one break their oath, the Keeper would come for them and take them to his dark realm of shadow and death.

"It is done," the giant announced, binding his hand. "Rest well Ranger, for when morning comes, the hunt begins."

"I pray I won't disappoint," Finn replied wryly.

The giant narrowed his eyes, lowering his gaze to the Ranger's wounded leg. "If you prove as tenacious as you have, then I'm certain you will not."

The giant mounted up, steadying himself in his saddle. Finn stepped back; eyes locked on the frost giant's dragon. There was a glint in the dragon's eyes. A strange flicker of hope. Finn cocked an eyebrow, as the feeling that much more was taking place than he could see.

***

"Draw them in! Hit, then fade!" Ard commanded.

The horses were tiring where the giants were not. Four of them had fallen. The poison had done its work. Still, arrows were few and needed to be used sparingly. The giants had made effective use of their shield wall, advancing, and defending as needed. They left few gaps in their defense, but this was to be expected.

It was a war of attrition and so far; they were winning. Four rangers had closed in to their right flank, as the archers took careful shots. The goal was to get them to make an opening. The ploy had worked, but they hit far fewer giants than desired.

Two of the Rangers went down in a flash. Their horses were like large dogs to the giants in comparison. A couple of them had held onto their spears, giving them far greater reach than the riders. But for each ranger lost, their odds of survival dwindled rapidly. Though the numbers were equal before the start of the engagement, one giant was worth four rangers in comparison.

Finn clenched his horses' reins as he and the other rangers circled them. *Henrik, if you'd only share your secrets with us. Dire wolves would make quick work of these brutes.*

The giants rarely invaded the old Thran's lands. As the longest lived among the Thran, the leaders of Sokoras, his reputation was legendary. The giants called him 'All-Father Naesir', after their forbearer. To them, Henrik's ferocity was the purest example of what all warriors should aspire to become.

"Where is he!" Finn overheard Ard shout. "Where is the bastard?!"

Finn's heart clenched in his chest. *No, Ard, stay focused. They're going to break formation soon. They can see our horses are tired. We need to wait for that moment and scatter and let the archers pick them off.*

No sooner had the thought taken shape, and the giants broke ranks, exploding like a beehive disturbed. "Archers, open fire," he called. "Brothers, scatter!" In the moment, a wave of relief washed over Finn. His brothers had listened. With everything so chaotic, most probably thought Ard had given the order. He was the highest ranked in the group. Arrows pelted their enemies, clipping or landing squarely where their flesh was exposed.

In the mad rush, four more Rangers fell, but not before two had gravely wounded two of their attackers. *The scales are balancing...* The thought made Finn's stomach turn, but it was the truth. Two giants for four rangers was a better trade. By the look of the others six more would fall to the poison in minutes. The tally was up to ten now, with six of their own lost.

A rage filled cry sounded and Finn's heart sank as he wheeled his horse in its direction. Ard had found his enemy, and the giant with the leg brace turned to meet him. He shouted out something in Ard's direction and the other giants scattered, as if giving birth for a deadly duel.

"Archers...!" Finn cried out, but was too late... their pair were too close and the risk of hitting Ard was too great.

A guttural shout drew the Ranger's attention as two giants barreled toward him. He reached for the skeggox cradled on his saddle and hurled it at an angle at one. The giant went to deflect it, but was too slow and it met the brute squarely in the face.

Spurring his horse, he glided past the other, and turned, drawing his sword, and slashing at the brute's back. The blade bit in, cutting across the chain links of his armor, but leaving a shallow wound. The giant roared in response and whirled about, sword cleaving the air.

It forced Finn to roll off the back of his horse as the large blade sliced through where his torso had been, cleaving his horse's head from its body. Staggering to his feet, the giant towered over him, sword and shield at the ready.

Watch his movements, Finn told himself. Frost giants were quicker than their frames made them appear, but they always moved wider when striking.

The giant reared his sword arm back, keeping his shield close to his chest. Finn stepped inside his swing, coming up under his arm, and thrust his sword into the brute's side. Again, it was another shallow wound, barely cutting the links of the brute's chain armor. Still, the giant stepped back, but not before it swung its shield arm against Finn's body.

The impact took the Ranger off his feet, sending him tumbling across the snow. The din of the fighting dulled to a strange echo as he pulled himself up. His body was numb, but instinct said he was still holding his sword.

A howl drew his attention, and he looked up to see the giant he'd been fighting with an arrow in its neck. Shaking his head clear, Finn took advantage of the opening and charged. The giant was too slow; the poison was already taking effect.

He slipped between the brute's legs, cutting along the groin, and stabbing at the back of its knee. The blade bit deep this time and the frost giant fell forward. Finn then took his sword and hamstrung his enemy, leaving him to flounder on the ground and focused his attention on the status of the battle.

"Go ahead!" Ard shouted. "Finish it!"

Finn turned, his mouth falling open as he screamed his friend's name. Ard was on his knees, his right arm hacked off as the frost giant with the leg brace held his enormous sword to the ranger's throat. It took no effort on the giant's part as he thrust the sword forward, decapitating Ard. Enraged, Finn charged when something struck him from behind and everything went black.

***

Finn awoke with a start, the sun's blaring rays stabbing through the trees as he got his bearings. He glanced to his left, seeing the makeshift sled he'd cobbled together. "Another dream." A soft howl echoed through the pinewood forest, and Finn turned in its direction.

Just above the hill, he saw a large dire wolf staring him down several yards away. Its coat was so white that if not for the swaying of its tail, he never would have noticed it. Cautiously, he reached for the giant's axe on the sled, sliding it from underneath the bear pelt covering it. The dire wolf stood motionless, then strangely bowed its head and turned to leave.

He blinked in disbelief, wondering if infection had indeed set into his leg. *Have you actually been watching me, Great Lady? No, that's not it.*

Saer often spoke of spirits and the wolves associated with them. But they were just legends and fairy tales. But she was fond of such stories, even if they were a bit too fanciful.

Noting how much the sun had already risen, Finn gathered up his things, taking only what he needed. He eyed the sled, knowing it would only slow him down, and quickly filled himself up on the cold bear meat he had stored in the snow before turning in for the night.

Then, gathering the remaining provisions, mostly nuts and bark, he headed west, his heart holding out for home.

Hours passed and still there was no sign of the giant or his dragon. The forest was eerily quiet and occasionally he would see the white dire wolf off in the distance. *Are you hunting me?*

It was a question he'd pondered many times. It was hard not to think The Lady was truly watching out for him. *Saer, you always teased about how there is more to this world than I think. Maybe you're right...* A soft wind blew, the chill nipping at his cheeks.

"Aren't I always right, dearest?"

Finn froze, lifting his eyes to a grouping of trees. His heart jumped, the joy of seeing his wife overwhelming him. "Saer?"

His wife smiled. "Who else would I be?"

He gazed to his right, at the distant line of trees where the dire wolf had been. The beast was gone. Finn cautiously stepped away. "This is a Death Dream. You're not here."

"No, my love, this is not a Death Dream."

Desperately wanting to believe his eyes, Finn's heart wavered. He inched closer, the haft of the giant's axe gripped firmly in his hand. "You can't be here. He'll kill us both."

"Then you must run, so he will not catch us."

"I am, as fast as I can," Finn said, tearing up. "He has a dragon. How do I outrun that?"

"How does a fox hide from the bear or the wolf?"

Fin paused. "He outwits them."

His wife nodded. "Now hurry, my lovely fox. He comes!"

Finn rushed past her and at his back, a draconic roar rang far in the distance. *He'll be tracking me by scent.*

Rushing to a cluster of trees, he pulled out his spark stones. Using the skeggox, he cut bark from one pine, digging into the dryer layers underneath. With the shiv and bear claws, he shaved away some of the wood, leaving it barely attached to the tree itself.

"I hope this works," he mumbled under his breath, and used the stone to set the pine tree on fire. It took a moment, but the tree lit up, the fire slowly eating away at the dryer wood. He then set out to do the same to the other trees. Another roar echoed, much closer than before. Time was almost up, but as he lit the last tree, Finn saw his plan was working. The trees were close enough to ignite their neighbors, and while some didn't fully burn, the smell of the needles and wet wood filled the air.

The sound of wings cutting the air caught his ears, and with no time left, Finn buried himself in the snow. Trees snapped around him, filtering through the powder covering him and he trembled at the dragon's heavy footsteps. When the snow beside grew more compact, he nearly gasped. The dragon was right on top of him.

"Clever, human!" the giant roared, starting a large fire to confuse my girl. "Let's see how far you've gotten in this mess." He barked a command in his own tongue and Finn heard the dragon breath in deeply. It was like listening to a blacksmith's bellows.

Upon exhaling, the crackle of the fire consuming the trees stopped, but the dragon had yet to move. The giant spoke again, and the dragon replied with a dull hiss. He groaned, as if annoyed, then the pair took to the skies, and all was still.

"That's twice, giant... I know that won't work again, but I've at least bought myself some time."

Waiting a little longer as the cold, wet snow seeped into his clothes, Finn unburied himself. He stole a glance at the trees he'd set aflame. Each sat covered with ice and frost. The dragon had used her deadly breath to quench the fire, though the area still reeked of charred wood and pine smoke.

Fin turned his attention to the west, then to the sky. The sun was two marks past its zenith. "Still more ground to cover."

Grabbing some burnt wood, he smeared it on himself and pocketed the charcoal fragments in one of the hide pouches he'd crafted. "I'll have to be more clever."

Night came quickly, as did the cold. Finn built himself a fire and set several snares around his camp. Through the night and between brief rests, he checked the snares, hoping to have caught something. Three of the eight had caught snowshoe rabbits, and he once again offered a prayer of thanks to The Lady.

Taking the charred wood, he smeared it all over each rabbit, making sure they reeked of its smell. Afterward, Finn set them free. When Morning came, he checked each again. Two more rabbits had gotten themselves caught, and taking fresh coals from his campfire, Finn covered them as well.

"Just buying time," he whispered.

For the rest of the day, he saw neither the dire wolf nor the heard the dragon and its rider. Taking it as a sign, he set more snares, gaining little sleep, but releasing four more rabbits into the night covered in ash.

As he fell asleep, Fin took mental stock of his remaining provisions. "One more day," he muttered. "That's all I have left."

Upon morning, he resumed his journey and still there was no sign of the dire wolf or his enemy. By midday, the skys grew more gloomy as the cloud cover worsened. The sun was hard to glimpse until, after another hour; it vanished completely. "I'm almost home," he said, clearing the treeline as his eyes fell on an open field of snow. But when he scanned the sea of white, Finn finally understood why he hadn't seen his enemy.

Both giant and dragon stood waiting in the distance. There would be no escape. The area was too open and the trees behind them too far. His enemy wasn't mounted, and the dragon lay curled up lazily like a cat waiting for its master on a porch.

The giant approached, axe ready, and Finn, with nowhere to run, met him halfway. His limp was more noticeable. "Well met, Ranger."

"Well met, Giant."

"Einar," the giant replied.

"Finn."

The giant smiled. "It is my honor to slay you, Finn. Your rabbit trick frustrated my poor girl to no end. You do not disappoint. It is a shame you aren't a frost giant. You'd be welcome in my hall."

"I wish I could offer the same. You killed a friend of mine."

The giant's face became like stone. "You've slain many of mine, as well. Now, do you yield, or do we fight?"

"We fight. I'll not be slaughtered like some yak for an evening meal."

There was a hint of regret in the giant's eye. "Truly an honor, Finn."

The giant widened his stance. His dragon tilted her head, one eye partly open. He held his massive skeggox in both hands, not bothering to pull the shield from his back. Finn readied his own weapon, though it was untested for him. He'd always preferred the sword. The giant looked as if he knew his own weapon well. The way he brandished his axe spoke of someone who had seen countless battles with it.

Wide arcs, Fin told himself. *I need to take advantage of that.*

As if sounding a bell, Einar's dragon loosed a mighty roar, and the giant rushed in, his axe swiftly cleaving the air. Finn nearly misstepped trying to avoid it, falling back to get beyond Einar's reach.

Einar was favoring his left leg. His limp had gotten worse. Something was off. As if... Finn's eyes widened. *He's been poisoned. But how had he survived for so this long?*

Finding courage in this knowledge, Finn waited for an opening, keeping his distance. Einar was tiring much too soon. But something felt wrong about simply wearing his enemy down. The frost giant had given him the greatest of respect and courtesy. So much to the degree that even a Sokoran would be insulted if they did not return it in kind.

So, Finn charged, axe readied, and to his surprise, Einar smiled. The ranger glided underneath the giant's swing, a rush of air blasting his face in the axe's wake. He spun, pouring all his strength into cleaving the leg harness holding Einar up, and to his satisfaction, the axe sliced through the leather straps keeping it in place.

Einar lost his balance, but not before backhanding Finn. Finn flew back, sliding across the snow as the air left his lungs. Something felt wrong, and he assumed one or more of his ribs were cracked. He pulled himself up, sharp pains stabbing at his side.

His skeggox lay several feet away between him and Einar. Einar was sweating now, his leg brace ruined, forcing him to use his axe like a cane for balance. A howl sounded behind Finn, and he turned to see the white dire wolf that had been following him standing at the treeline.

Fin reached behind him, where the bone shiv he made lay tucked into his trousers. "One strike," he whispered. Einar smiled, as if the frost giant had read his mind.

Clutching his side, Finn ran at Einar, and the giant pulled himself up, balancing on his good leg to meet him. He swung, the skeggox coming in lower this time. Finn stopped short, spinning counter to the swing, and rushing up to Einar's right leg, stabbing the bone shiv into the tendon at his heel.

Einar howled, collapsing face first under his own momentum into the snow. He rolled over and laughed. "I yield," he announced. "Finish me with honor and let me enter All-Father Naesir's halls with dignity."

"It doesn't feel right. You were poisoned," Finn replied.

Einar coughed. The fever was taking hold. "I've survived far longer than the others. I've tried every cure, even magic. Whatever this is, you Sokorans have frightened many of the tribes among my people. Your friend was clever to lace his blade with it."

Ard... so you won in the end. Finn walked toward his skeggox lay and picked it up, but as he turned to face Einar, the white wolf stood between them. It turned, eyes locked on the dragon, and bowed its head.

"The agreement is done," the dragon announced. "I have delivered and am now free."

The dire wolf drew closer to Einar, and a fog settled over them. Moments later, they were gone. Finn could only stare. What is this?

Einar's dragon rose, stalking closer. "Frustvivla," she said. "You are now my master, unless I am to be freed..."

There was a way she said things that hinted not as if it were a question, but a veiled demand. "What did I witness?" Finn asked.

"A pact forged, and a promise kept," the dragon replied. "Now, what shall we do?"

"I wasn't aware your kind even spoke."

The frost dragon smirked. At least that's what it appeared like. "Little thing, there is much in this world you do not know and more you are not meant to. So, I ask again, what shall we do?"

"I just want to go home. After that, I do not care."

"Then home it shall be and then I will be free."

Finn nodded. It was clear now she wasn't making a suggestion. "Then home it shall be and afterward you will be free."